Harrison had been my assistant since I'd gotten here. I hadn't picked him and hadn't asked questions. Whoever picked him had made a good choice.

What I did know was that he was my age and had an architectural degree from the University of Houston. Though it wasn't part of my job description, I planned to begin mentoring him after I got a handle on my own projects.

I also knew that he was far too handsome with deep blue eyes that always seemed to hold a secret smile. By the end of the day he had a five o'clock shadow that added a bad boy sheen to his boy next door looks.

Not that I noticed. He was my assistant. And work was not a dating pool.

With nothing of interest in my email, I locked the phone and tapped a finger against the screen.

"Do you know what this meeting is about?" I asked.

"No ma'am," he said, with a glance in my direction. "You don't?"

"Nuh-uh."

Finally, Mr. Fleming walked in and sat at his desk.

He was always a pleasant man, but at the moment he was wearing a scowl.

I braced myself, for what, I didn't know.

"I've been on the phone all morning," he said, without preamble.

"Is something wrong with the Martin account?" I'd been working on the Martin account since I got here four months ago.

It was a planned mid-rise condominium unit near the Highland shopping center in River Oaks. A labor of love for me. Everything I believed in. *Less is more*. Comfortable housing, designed especially for those who worked from home. No gold faucets that were prohibitive to using. Just high quality and clean lines.

"I'm afraid I have some bad news."

Why hadn't Mr. Martin come to me? If there was a problem with the designs, he should have come to me.

"I can fix it," I said. "He should have come to me."

"It isn't Mr. Martin's account."

I glanced over at Harrison. He shook his head almost imperceptibly.

I forced a smile that I was certain looked fake.

"I don't understand—"

"You're being deported," Mr. Fleming said.

"What? Why? I don't—"

"Your Visa expired."

"No," I said. "I renewed it. I have a letter. The paperwork is in progress."

"I'm sorry," he said. "It was denied."

I inhaled deeply. I could still fix this.

"Okay," I said. "I'll just go to Vancouver for six months. Work remotely. I can reapply and come right back."

Mr. Fleming was shaking his head.

"I already proposed that. They said no."

"You don't know how this..." I said. "I'll go to the Immigration office. Straighten it all out."

"Emma," he said. "This is serious. I bought you twelve hours. They were coming to arrest you."

A knot formed in the pit of my stomach. I'd seen the police car myself. I put a hand to my waist to brace myself.

"Arrest? But... I..." I didn't do anything wrong. I went to work every day. I worked hard.

I hadn't set foot in Canada since the day I'd left for college. Going back to Vancouver wasn't an option. My architectural license was here. In the states.

"I agreed to put you on a flight to Vancouver and fly you there myself."

"They can't do that," Harrison said, speaking up suddenly.

I looked at Harrison. I didn't even think he liked me all that much, but here he was going to bat for me.

UNEXPECTED VOWS

UNEXPECTED VOWS

THE WORTHINGTONS

KATHRYN KALEIGH

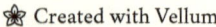

To learn more about Kathryn Kaleigh, visit

www.kathrynkaleigh.com

Kathryn Kaleigh

1

EMMA BLAKE

*T*oday was going to be a good day.

April weather in Houston was stunningly beautiful. It was still winter in a lot of the country and all of Canada. Take Vancouver, for instance. Today was rainy with a high of thirty-five degrees.

I parked in my assigned spot in the second floor of the garage, grabbed my oversized tote bag and Starbuck's latte, and took the elevator down to the ground floor. I was early, as always, so I was the only one on the elevator. I liked it that way. It was one of the many ways that I avoided small talk.

The door opened and I stepped out, my red-bottomed heels tapping on the concrete. The shoes pinched my feet and scraped the backs of my ankles, but image was everything. Tonight I would reward myself with a hot bath and soak away the soreness. Then tomorrow I would do it all over again.

I could have turned left and walked inside, using the staff elevator to get to my office. Instead, I turned right toward the visitor's entrance. Using the sidewalk allowed me to soak up a few minutes of sunshine before I spent the rest of the day tucked away in my air-conditioned office. Two butterflies flitted around the row of pink and white daisies lining the walkway while a bluebird did a touch and go over one of the half dozen wooden benches.

The usual food truck called *Morning and Noon* sat in its usual place in the parking lot. They had THE best egg and cheese biscuits and lattes that were as good as the one in my hand. Although there was no line yet, I didn't stop. Not having to get my own breakfast or lunch was one of the perks of being a Senior Architect.

"Good morning, Miss Blake," Bob, the doorman said as he opened the door for me.

"Good morning, Bob. Is Harrison here yet?"

I already knew that he wasn't, but I liked Bob. He was a good man.

"No ma'am. Not yet. He'll be here though."

"Uh huh." I slid my shades up to the top of my head and walked inside. "I know." The receptionist, Misty, liked those scented humidifiers, so the lobby always smelled like cinnamon or vanilla and spruce trees during December.

"Have a good day," Bob said.

"You too, Bob."

I pushed the button to go up to the tenth floor. My employer, Skye Designs, occupied floors ten and eleven. There was only one more floor above that—the Skye Travels corporate office. They were the least busy since their main office was at the airport. A waste of good space, but no one asked me.

One of my associates had designed a rooftop work and lounge area and was waiting on board approval. I'd seen the plans and was looking forward to having the outdoor space to use as a place to take a break from my desk. Taking a cue from Las Vegas, he was proposing using an outdoor misting system. With the Houston weather as hot as it was during the long summer months, those misting systems were becoming more and more popular. In fact, I was proposing private patio misting systems as part of my current project design.

Stepping off the elevator, I walked down the hallway to my corner office and dropped my tote bag on my desk. Taking my coffee, I went to the window and looked out over the Uptown Galleria area. This building was on the western edge of River Oaks, giving me a south and west view.

I'd lived in New York for all of eleven months before being recruited to Houston by Skye Designs. I'd established a good reputation based partly on my motto "Less is More." One of the Worthington Enterprises board members, a woman named Ainsley Beaufort, had purchased one of the New York condos based on my designs. She'd liked it so much, she'd offered me a job at her company in Houston.

It was hard to turn down a position as senior architect, especially with the salary they offered. But it wasn't New York, something I was still on the fence about.

A police car pulled up to front of the building and parking. I shrugged. Not my business.

Wanting to get some creative work done before my meetings started, I sat at my drafting desk and did some sketches.

HARRISON MOORE

*G*rabbing two egg and cheese biscuits and two lattes from the food truck outside the office, I glanced at my watch. I was still early enough.

As an executive assistant, if I wasn't early to work, I was late. And I had to come with breakfast in hand or there would be hell to pay.

"Good morning, Bob," I said as I hurried through the door he held open.

"Boss is upstairs." Bob's voice held a note of warning.

"I had no doubt," I said over my shoulder, heading toward the elevators.

I punched the button with my elbow and took a taste of my coffee. Not bad. I usually preferred my coffee cold, but it easier to just order two hot coffees.

Getting on the elevator, I punched eleven with my elbow and nearly spilled coffee.

I squared my shoulders and waited for the doors to open.

The tenth floor, like the rest of the two-year-old building was plush and understated. Worthington Enterprises was expanding so quickly and in so many different directions, they had decided to form a corporation and build their own building to house the myriad divisions they were developing.

The top floor was occupied by Skye Travels. The legendary founder of the Skye Travels airline company, Noah Worthington, still came into the office on occasion. And even though it was only on occasion, he had the best office in the building.

A perk of being the founder.

The tenth and eleventh floors belonged to Skye Designs. Founded by one of Noah's daughters, it was one of the newest and fastest growing architectural firms in the country. Texas was perfect for the Worthingtons. Go big or go home could be their motto.

That was one reason why I chose to work here. Another thing the Worthingtons believed in was starting from the ground up. Unless, of course, a person was like Emma Blake who brought their reputation with them.

If you start at the bottom, you know how things run from the inside out, Noah had told me on the day he'd hired me as an executive assistant.

I dropped off one coffee and one biscuit at my desk and knocked on Emma's door.

"Come," she said.

I rolled my eyes. Would it seriously hurt her to say *come in* instead of *come?*

"Good morning, Miss Emma," I said.

She didn't bother to glance up from her protractor.

"Breakfast is on your table," I said as I set the coffee and biscuit on the little table next to one of the floor-to-ceiling windows. Why she didn't work there, I didn't know. If this were ever my office, I'd put my drafting table right in front of this window.

I shrugged when she didn't respond and walked back out.

"Thank you," she said, just before I closed the door behind me.

Emma wasn't all that bad. She expected five hundred percent from everyone, including herself. Always first to arrive in the mornings and last to leave at night, she had no social life. In the four months I'd worked for her, I'd never once recorded a social engagement on her calendar. No personal phone calls. Nothing. Just work. Notwithstanding her hairstylist, personal trainer and nutritionist.

The oddest part about her lack of a social life was that she was a looker. Five four, one hundred twenty pounds, long brunette hair secured at the back of her head with a clip. A heart-shaped face with emerald green eyes and perfectly bow-shaped lips.

Always dressed professionally, I'd never seen her without a suit jacket. And heels. The woman always wore heels.

Sitting at my own desk I ate my breakfast while I checked messages and reviewed her calendar.

Maybe, just maybe, I'd have a few minutes to work on my own project today while she was in a meeting.

Just as I was caught up, a message popped up on my screen.

EMMA: *I need you in my meeting this morning.*

So much for that. I didn't know how I was supposed to ever be successful with my own project if I was always running after Emma Blake.

EMMA

*M*y assistant, Harrison Moore, sat next to me with his iPad open and ready to take notes while we waited for Mr. Jackson Fleming.

Mr. Fleming had a large corner office on the eleventh floor with a perfect view of downtown Houston. He had this office in Houston and one at the airport. He wasn't an architect. He was a pilot.

But he and his wife had founded Skye Designs, so there was no one to complain to about how the office could be better used by someone who worked there every day. Besides, he was the head of Skye Designs.

I used the wait time to check my emails.

"Did you follow up on this question from Robert Johnson?"

"Yes ma'am," Harrison said.

Harrison had been my assistant since I'd gotten here. I hadn't picked him and hadn't asked questions. Whoever picked him had made a good choice.

What I did know was that he was my age and had an architectural degree from the University of Houston. Though it wasn't part of my job description, I planned to begin mentoring him after I got a handle on my own projects.

I also knew that he was far too handsome with deep blue eyes that always seemed to hold a secret smile. By the end of the day he had a five o'clock shadow that added a bad boy sheen to his boy next door looks.

Not that I noticed. He was my assistant. And work was not a dating pool.

With nothing of interest in my email, I locked the phone and tapped a finger against the screen.

"Do you know what this meeting is about?" I asked.

"No ma'am," he said, with a glance in my direction. "You don't?"

"Nuh-uh."

Finally, Mr. Fleming walked in and sat at his desk.

He was always a pleasant man, but at the moment he was wearing a scowl.

I braced myself, for what, I didn't know.

"I've been on the phone all morning," he said, without preamble.

"Is something wrong with the Martin account?" I'd been working on the Martin account since I got here four months ago.

It was a planned mid-rise condominium unit near the Highland shopping center in River Oaks. A labor of love for me. Everything I believed in. *Less is more*. Comfortable housing, designed especially for those who worked from home. No gold faucets that were prohibitive to using. Just high quality and clean lines.

"I'm afraid I have some bad news."

Why hadn't Mr. Martin come to me? If there was a problem with the designs, he should have come to me.

"I can fix it," I said. "He should have come to me."

"It isn't Mr. Martin's account."

I glanced over at Harrison. He shook his head almost imperceptibly.

I forced a smile that I was certain looked fake.

"I don't understand—"

"You're being deported," Mr. Fleming said.

"What? Why? I don't—"

"Your Visa expired."

"No," I said. "I renewed it. I have a letter. The paperwork is in progress."

"I'm sorry," he said. "It was denied."

I inhaled deeply. I could still fix this.

"Okay," I said. "I'll just go to Vancouver for six months. Work remotely. I can reapply and come right back."

Mr. Fleming was shaking his head.

"I already proposed that. They said no."

"You don't know how this..." I said. "I'll go to the Immigration office. Straighten it all out."

"Emma," he said. "This is serious. I bought you twelve hours. They were coming to arrest you."

A knot formed in the pit of my stomach. I'd seen the police car myself. I put a hand to my waist to brace myself.

"Arrest? But... I..." I didn't do anything wrong. I went to work every day. I worked hard.

I hadn't set foot in Canada since the day I'd left for college. Going back to Vancouver wasn't an option. My architectural license was here. In the states.

"I agreed to put you on a flight to Vancouver and fly you there myself."

"They can't do that," Harrison said, speaking up suddenly.

I looked at Harrison. I didn't even think he liked me all that much, but here he was going to bat for me.

4

HARRISON

*E*mma and I rode the elevator down one floor in silence. Everyone else was busy at work, hardly even glancing up as we walked past.

I knew everyone by name. Knew things about them. Spouses. Kids. Emma had been here for four months and she hardly knew anyone.

I had to start working her out of that. Find ways to slowly introduce her to people. She was introverted as hell and sometimes an introvert needed help getting to know people. If she was going to work here, she needed to have friends.

"Do you want to go to the Immigration office now?" I asked, checking my watch.

She squared her shoulders. "Yes. I don't have much time."

"Agreed."

I didn't ask her how this had happened. I could have taken care of the paperwork myself. In fact... I was surprised she didn't ask me to do it. I did everything else.

While I waited for her to grab the strappy handbag she carried in her tote bag, I pulled up directions to the Immigration office. Memorized it.

"Ready?" I asked when she came back out.

She ran a hand over her skirt. "Yes."

Back down the elevator, down the hallway, and out to the garage.

"You drive," she said, handing me her keys.

"Sure," I said and opened the passenger door of her black Porsche Cayenne. She climbed in and put on her sunshades.

I walked around to the driver's side. She'd driven the few times we'd gone over to the construction site, so I took a minute to acquaint myself with her car.

She sat perfectly still, staring straight ahead, her hands clasped in her lap.

"Emma," I said.

Startled, she turned in my direction.

"It's going to be okay," I said. "I'm sure it's just a mix up."

"Jackson Fleming couldn't get it straightened out," she said. "And… they came to arrest me."

She was looking straight ahead again.

I backed up and headed out of the garage.

"We'll do whatever it takes," I said. "Besides. He isn't you."

A hint of a smile played about her lips.

I merged onto the freeway and we sat in traffic.

I couldn't say why, but I had a feeling there was something hidden behind her perfect coiffed hair and professional attire.

If she'd been any other woman, any one of my sisters or cousins, I would have reached out and put a hand over hers in comfort.

But instead, the most I could hope for was to distract her.

"Robert Johnson agreed with your ideas about flipping the kitchen and living room," I said. Architect Robert Johnson had asked Emma for a consult on the plans for a house he was building for a client. It had cost him a pretty penny, though. Emma didn't mind helping, but she didn't come cheap.

"That's good," she said, straightening in her seat. It opened the room up."

"Agreed. You thought they were good otherwise?"

"They were fine," she said. "There were some other things I might have done, but it works."

The conversation had the desired effect. She relaxed a little.

The cars started to move. Finally.

"We'll be there soon," I said.

*T*hree hours later after sitting in traffic and waiting in the crowded lobby of the Immigration office, we stepped out onto the sidewalk.

The sun was warm on my cheeks and a light breeze tugged a strand of hair loose and blew it across my face. I tucked it behind an ear and stood looking out toward the parking lot.

Harrison was focused on his iPad, reading something.

He'd been right. They'd been planning on arresting me, but he bought me twelve hours with the agreement that I would get on a plane at Skye Travels.

My paperwork had gotten lost somewhere in the bowels of the government system and there was no accounting for it.

If I could go back in time, I'd give it to Harrison to take of. He'd have tracked it and kept up with it, but I'd been stubborn. The paperwork had all my personal information on it and he already knew just about everything about the current me. I hadn't wanted him to know the past me, too.

Sometimes I got the idea that Harrison was amused by me and other times I thought he was afraid of me.

It had taken a bit of time to get used to having a personal

assistant, but I'd taken to it like a duck to water for the most part.

I tended to get lost in my work and sometimes tuned out everything around me. Probably made me seem rude and withdrawn.

"Well," I said. "I need to get my office packed." It felt like giving up, but going to prison was not a viable option. It was important to know when to lay down your arms and surrender.

So that's what I had to do. I'd regroup and figure out what to do next. There was always a solution. I just had to be creative and find it.

Harrison glanced over at me with a strange look on his face.

"You might have some other options you haven't considered."

"Like what?" I asked, my brows furrowed.

He closed the iPad and look straight into my eyes.

His eyes were blue with white shards shooting out from the center. I hadn't noticed that before.

"I need to make a phone call," he said, walking away from me, his phone pressed to his ear, so that I couldn't hear what he was saying.

He was pacing as he talked.

I turned my face up to the warmth of the sun and closed my eyes. Traffic raced by. Everyone in a hurry.

I wasn't one to give up. This was just a setback. That was all.

Harrison walked back toward me, his gaze pinned to mine.

Belatedly, I realized I was holding my breath.

My heart skipped a little as he walked toward me with purpose. I was being fanciful. He was my assistant.

He slid his phone back into his pocket.

"You have another option."

"What kind of option?" I asked, warily.

He put his hands on his hips and looked down at me. He

was a good head taller than I was. Somehow I had become accustomed to having him around and he gave me a feeling of security.

I realized in that instant just how well he'd been taking care of me over these past four months. He'd get me breakfast, lunch, and dinner. Made my appointments and made sure I kept them. He had my back at every turn.

I didn't trust a lot of people, but I trusted him.

"What?" I asked again.

"You can marry me."

HARRISON

I wasn't related to the founder of Worthington Enterprises—at least not by blood. But he was my mother's ex-husband. He and my mother remained on good terms over the years which made their lives easier seeing as how they had a daughter together—my half-sister.

Perhaps more importantly, Noah was my Godfather.

At any rate, Noah Worthington treated me like family. When I'd expressed an interest in architecture and went on to graduate with a degree in it from the University of Houston, he'd encouraged me to remain in Houston and go to work for the newest arm of Worthington Enterprises—Skye Designs.

He'd put me in the position of assistant to Emma Blake, a renowned architect they had recruited from New York. You'll learn a lot from her, Noah had said. From just being around her.

I hadn't disagreed and he was paying me as much as most of my fellow students were making as junior architects. Seemed like I couldn't go wrong.

But now Emma was being was deported for a mix-up in

paperwork. If I'd known about it, I'd have kept this from happening.

As it was, I used my connection with Noah to pull a couple of strings and I had found a solution to her problem—make her my wife.

There was just one caveat.

The wedding had to be today.

Right now Emma was looking at me like I'd sprung a leaky roof.

"I think I misunderstood you," she said. The breeze blew a strand of hair that had come loose from her hair clip across her face. I found that unsettlingly sexy.

"There's a loophole to keep you from having be deported."

She shook her head.

"You can get married," I said. "to an American." I waited a beat. "Me."

I pressed my fingertips against my brow. "I don't think so." There were too many stipulations about marriage. I vaguely remembered going through my initial orientation thinking that marriage was not an option. It had to be within so many days of this and so many days of that.

"I don't think… How did you—"

"I used my connections," I said. "There's an exception to every rule. It's all in who you know."

"And you know somebody."

"I know some people. I know a lot of people."

She shifted from one foot to the other. That hesitation told me she was considering it.

This was one of those things that I hadn't thought through. I'd just gone on instinct and impulse.

Putting her hands on her hips, she mirrored my stance.

"Why?" she asked, looking at me from beneath her lush, thick eyelashes.

Why indeed? I didn't have an answer for her. I merely went with what came to mind. I shrugged.

"Why not?"

EMMA

"I'll drive," I said, holding out my hand for the keys as I walked past Harrison.

I slid into the driver's seat and pressed the button to put the seat and mirrors back on my settings. Harrison climbed into the passenger's seat.

I needed something to take my mind off of everything. Even if just for a few minutes.

The drive back to the office went a lot quicker than the drive out had. Whether it was because there was less traffic or because my thoughts were swirling dangerously, I couldn't say.

Harrison texted someone, but otherwise we rode in silence back to the office.

I pulled into my parking space and put the car in park.

Then I just sat there. Stunned.

My brain slid everything into place backwards.

Most importantly, I needed to avoid being arrested. By flying out to Vancouver today, I would avoid that. So that wasn't a danger at this point.

Second, I would like to avoid being deported at all.

The government wasn't giving me any options. Leave or go to prison.

But now I'd been presented with another option.

Marry Harrison. My assistant.

I looked at him out of the corner of my eyes.

His fingers flew over the phone as he did whatever it was he does to remain incredibly efficient. I really didn't know that much—if anything—about him on a personal level. I'd known what I needed to know. He was a topnotch assistant.

At one point, I had reviewed his vita so I knew he had a degree in architectural design. I hadn't questioned why he was working as an assistant.

After graduation, I'd done all sorts of odd jobs in architectural firms, then started working my way up. One of those odd jobs had been working as a personal assistant.

So I'd seen nothing out of the ordinary.

"Do you have family in Vancouver?" he asked.

"What?" His question jarred me out of my head. "No."

"Friends?"

"I haven't been back since I left for college, so no. Nothing." I squeezed the leather steering wheel.

What would happen with my car? My condo? I *owned* things here. I was a tax paying citizen. They could just make me leave. I'd done nothing wrong.

But apparently they could.

Harrison stretched out his long legs. Tapped his phone against his thigh.

"It really is your best option," he said.

I turned and faced him.

Why would he upend his life like this for someone he barely knew?

He was a handsome man and everyone liked him.

"You don't have a girlfriend?"

"I'm always at work," he said, with a sideways grin.

I nodded and looked ahead again toward the white brick wall. I could vouch for that.

"What's the catch?"

He scrubbed his hands over his face. "Good question."

I knew there had to be a catch. If it was money he wanted, I had a good bit of savings. I never did anything other than work. I had a capsule wardrobe. Good pieces, but they served me well and kept my bank account happy.

"Two things," he said.

I braced myself. I'd heard horror stories about people being blackmailed for this sort of thing. Maybe Vancouver wasn't such a bad option after all. I'd gotten my license in the states. I could get one in Canada.

I'd figure out how to sell my house and car from there. Just not prison. Anything but prison.

"You give me time to work on my own project."

"What project?"

"I'm designing my high-end apartment complex."

"Okay." Time wasn't a problem. Sounded interesting anyway. "What's the other thing?"

"We tell my family it's real."

I looked at him again. Searched his eyes for some explanation.

"They won't believe us. Jackson could tell them."

"How would he know otherwise?"

"I don't think it'll work."

"Alright." He shrugged and looked away. "Then it's off the table. If we can't convince my family, then we'll both go to prison."

"I don't understand," I said. I tried to put myself in his shoes. Would I do it for him? I honestly couldn't say that I would.

"Why would you do this?"

HARRISON

*W*e sat in Emma's car in the parking garage at Worthington Enterprises. There were only half a dozen cars around us. I checked my watch. Where had the day gone? The only people left were the people like me and Emma who worked past noon on Friday afternoons.

Someone walked to one of the cars behind us, started up the motor, and drove off. Now it was quiet except for the roar of a blower cleaning just on the other side of the garage.

Emma's caution was justified, especially since I didn't know how to answer her. There was no logic in my offer to marry her.

Just a gut feeling that it was right. If I questioned it too much, logic would kick in and I would probably change my mind.

I was between girlfriends because... the whole work thing kept me too busy to bother looking.

I was being honest, though, when I said we had to convince my family that the marriage was real. If Immigrations came to investigate, they would nail us both for fraud.

My parents and siblings would believe me. They lived in

Los Angeles and I didn't get home to visit nearly often enough and even my phone calls had been brief lately. They would most likely see it as an explanation for why they didn't hear much from me.

The thought of Emma being deported made me sick to my stomach.

No matter how distant I found her, it brightened my day to see her. I hadn't given that much though until now. Maybe that was why I hadn't been worried about dating anyone.

"It wouldn't be real," I said. "I'm not asking for any strings other than the time. Convincing my family is just a necessary part of the deal."

She nodded. "Okay."

I waited patiently for all of three minutes. But patience was not one of my virtues.

"Come on," I said. "Let's walk outside."

While she released her seatbelt and gathered up her things, I went around and opened her door.

"Thank you," she said, stepping out the car.

I leaned back, but was still close enough that I could still smell the clean, fresh scent of her hair—a swirl of lavender and vanilla.

I took a step back before I followed my instinct to release the clip at the back of her head and bury my hands in the long strands of her hair.

Clearing my throat, I turned and, after she stepped out of the way, closed the car door.

She followed me outside the garage to the sidewalk that led to the front door.

"Sit here?" I asked, indicating the bench with a nod. I was used to doing what Emma asked. This suddenly flipping of roles was a little unsettling. Certainly unexpected.

She sat down and sitting next to her, I leaned forward, my elbows on my thighs.

The food truck was packing up, getting ready to leave for the day. They'd come back tomorrow and do it all over again.

"What are you thinking?" I asked.

She inhaled on a ragged breath. "I don't know what to think. To be quite honest, I'm overwhelmed."

"It's a lot to consider."

Though, in my mind, it was fairly straight forward. Marry me or be deported to Vancouver. I'd already decided that I wasn't leaving Texas unless something unforeseen happened. So it was a no brainer for me.

If I was her, I'd do it.

Then it occurred to that she might not want to marry me.

She could have a secret boyfriend. Or maybe she just didn't like me well enough.

It wasn't like she knew anything about me.

"What's making you hesitate?" I asked.

She glanced with at me with an odd expression. "It's a huge thing."

"So is being deported."

She nodded slowly.

"You want some coffee?" I asked.

"Sure."

Giving her a minute to herself, I walked over to the food truck and ordered two coffees.

She leaned her head up, turning her face toward the sun.

Emma truly was beautiful. But she was an ice princess. I was crazy to offer to marry her.

I shrugged it off.

I paid for the coffees and carried them back, handing one to Emma.

"Thank you," she said, taking the cup from her.

Was a portion, however small, of the ice princess thawing?

I sat next to her again and sipped the hot coffee.

"It's a simple business arrangement," I said.

She nodded and glanced at me. "I know."

"We only have to remain married for two years."

"Two years," she scoffed.

"It's okay," I said. "I understand you may be in a relationship."

"With who?" she asked, looking at me, her brow arched delicately.

I laughed. "I don't know. A secret man who doesn't contact you at work... and that you never see."

"I'm not," she said.

"I'd say take your time. Think about it. But, there's no time. You have to pack up and get to the airport."

She clutched the coffee cup like a lifeline between both hands.

"Tell me how this would work," she said.

This was most definitely progress.

I ignored the butterflies in my stomach.

It was a big deal for me, too.

9

EMMA

*I*t was late in the day. That time before the sun began its downward descent toward the horizon. The time when sometimes, like today, the moon was visible.

Was it a sign that the sun and the moon were both visible at the same time?

A sign of something changing? Something good, perhaps?

I'd gone from Boston to New York to Houston and though I liked all three of those cities for different reasons, Houston was by far my favorite city so far.

Did it have anything to do with the man sitting next to me?

I caught myself looking forward to seeing him in the mornings and sometimes thinking about him at night. Mostly thinking about work things, but still... he was interwoven with my job here so much that I couldn't separate the two.

When I thought of work, I thought of Harrison.

"You'd move in with me," he said.

"Why not my place?" I asked, thinking of the condo I'd barely had time to move into. I just now had things like I wanted them.

"Because it makes good sense. My place is bigger and I'm established."

"How do you know your place is bigger?"

"You might recall the Saturday I brought you lunch."

"Right." I did recall. I'd been playing around with a project and got caught up in it. It had been a cold January day with sleet in the forecast. I'd texted Harrison for information and he'd ended up bringing over some blueprints.

"Anyway, we'll move into my place."

"So you want me to sell my place?"

He shrugged. "Not necessarily. You could keep it. Rent it."

"So I could move back in it."

He glanced at me, set his coffee down, and leaning back.

"After the two years." I clarified.

"That's the thing," he said, looking at me now. "You've got to put that out of your head."

"How am I supposed to do that?"

"Don't think about it being temporary. If you think about it way, you'll say something that'll tip people off."

I pressed my hands against my temples.

"There's no way to pull this off today."

"The longer we wait, the more true that is." He glanced at his watch. "I've got to get in touch with a judge and an attorney to draw up the contract."

"You just shouldn't think about it being temporary."

He grinned at me. "It's complicated."

A butterfly landed on the back of my hand. Holding my breath, I slowly lifted my hand while the butterfly moved its wings up and down.

My grandmother used to say that butterflies were good luck.

If you're fortunate enough for a butterfly to land on you, good fortune will be bestowed on you, she'd said.

"Okay," I said, looking at Harrison. "Let's do it."

"Really?"

His expression was so boyishly charming, it nearly took my breath away.

This is just business.

This is just business.

If I kept repeating it to myself, it would be true.

Right?

10

HARRISON

*A*s the evening sun began to set, casting a splatter of orange and red across the sky, I paced in my office, my phone on speaker.

First I called Noah. He was the only person I told the truth to and was the only one I ever would tell.

It didn't take long to get him on board.

"I need to tell Savannah," he said.

That was the thing about secrets...

"Okay," I said. I knew that Noah and Savannah were inseparable. I also figured that Savannah could help him pull things together more quickly.

And time was of the essence.

Most women would have spent the next two hours shopping for a wedding dress.

Emma, however, used the time to return a call from Robert Johnson.

I just shook my head.

It was my job to take care of her anyway.

With Noah and Savannah on my side, it took no time to pull things together.

Judge Benson would be arriving at six o'clock, marriage certificate in hand.

Noah and Savannah would serve as witnesses.

No one else needed to be involved.

Not even Jackson Fleming. It had gone beyond him now anyway.

When everything was in place, I stuck my head in her door.

"The wedding's at six," I said.

"Okay," she said, looking up from her drafting table.

"Is there anyone you want to call?"

"No," she said.

I took a step inside her office door.

"Are you going to wear that?"

She glanced down at her black pencil skirt and matching jacket. She wore a white blouse underneath it.

"What's wrong with this?" she asked.

"Well," I said, putting my hands on my hips. "It's a wedding."

"But it's not a real—"

He held up a hand to stop me in mid-sentence.

"We're going to sign the papers," he said. "in a few minutes. Then we're going to have a real wedding."

She nodded slowly and ran her fingertip along her pencil.

"Alright," she said.

"Do you want to go home and change?"

"I don't have anything other than black."

"Yes, you do," I said. "You have that taupe suit."

She shook her head.

"It has an ink stain on it."

She bent her head back to the drawing on her desk.

We were about to get married, for God's sake.

I went over and slid the pencil out of her hand.

"Hey," she said. "I was—"

"It'll wait. We're going to Nordstrom's."

"But I—"

I looked at her crossways.

"When they come and look at the pictures for evidence, they need to see you wearing a wedding dress."

"I—"

"I'm not going to prison because you can't stop working for one damn hour."

"Fine," she said, pushing back from the table.

I grabbed her handbag and tossed it over my shoulder.

"We don't have much time," I said, holding out a hand for her.

11

EMMA

*W*e took Harrison's car to Nordstrom's. I'd never been in his car. I'd expected something old and maybe ragged. He was fresh out of college, after all.

But he drove a black Land Rover SUV. Like my car, it still carried that new car smell.

Wondering how an assistant could afford such a luxury car distracted me from being cross at him for dragging me away from work.

He didn't understand that the way I was coping with all of this was by burying my head in work.

I didn't have anyone to call. No family.

My parents had died when I was fifteen and I'd lived with my grandmother for the next three years. She'd died while I was in college.

So there was no one. No one to call. No one to tell. No one to share what was supposed to be an exciting time in my life.

I just didn't feel like telling Harrison all that right now.

Traffic was bad on the way to the Galleria, but Harrison navigated it like a pro.

He'd dropped the car off with the valet and we walked inside together.

The store smelled like cologne and new clothes.

Harrison knew where to go. We went straight up the escalators to the third floor.

My breath hitched when I saw the wedding dress section and I nearly stumbled.

We were really doing this.

I lifted my chin. This was a business deal and it was going to keep me in the states.

I did what I had to do. I'd always taken care of myself for as long as I could remember and this was just another step along that path.

A middle-age woman, named Bree, according to her name tag greeted us with a smile.

"Good evening," she said. "Are you two here to look at wedding gowns?"

"We actually need to buy one," Harrison said.

"Of course. When do you need it?"

Harrison glanced at his watch. "No more than an hour from now."

"Oh," Bree said. "We need at least a week. Two would be better."

Harrison reached into his jacket pocket and pulled out a black credit card. Handing it to her.

Bree's eyes widened when she looked at it.

"Of course, Mr. Moore," she said. "You just find what you like and we'll take care of it. You look around while I call the seamstress. To make sure she's still here."

"Thank you," Harrison said, guiding me toward the racks of white dresses.

While I stood there, dumbfounded, still wondering what was happening, Harrison looked through the racks of dresses.

He pulled out a mermaid dress, held it out.

"This one might do," he said.

Then Bree was there, taking the dress from him.

"Follow me to the dressing room," she said. "Miss?" She looked questioningly at me.

"Emma," I said.

"Miss Emma." I followed her into a huge dressing room with mirrors all around. She led me behind a maroon velvet curtain and starting unbuttoning the gown.

"This one might just fit you," she said. "without too many adjustments."

"I can get it," I said, setting my handbag on the bench.

"I'll help you," she insisted.

"No, really," I said. "I can do it."

Bree reluctantly left me behind the curtain, but she didn't go far. I could feel her standing back there.

I stepped out of my shoes, then slipped out of my jacket and stepped out of my skirt. I carefully folded my clothes and set them aside.

I looked at the volumes of white organza and silk hanging in front of me and wondered whether it was supposed to go over my head or was I supposed to step into it?

I decided it probably went over my head to keep it off the floor as much as possible.

I spent a few minutes lost in the volumes of silk before I found my way out.

But, for the life of me, I couldn't fasten the back. So many tiny buttons and clasps that I just could not reach.

Giving up, I stepped out from behind the curtain.

"Can you help me?" I asked.

12

HARRISON

I paced the floor, waiting for Emma to come out of the dressing room.

I'd sent two more dresses back via Bree. One of them had to be the right dress. It didn't have to be perfect... although... perfect would be good.

The air was scented with flowers and the music was soft and romantic. All geared toward the women getting married for love.

But people got married for all sorts of reasons and not all of them had anything to do with love.

A marriage was a business contract... with paperwork... Maybe it should be viewed for what it was. Business.

I knew exactly what I was doing. I was justifying my decision to marry Emma.

Not for love, but for business.

Could I have married her for love? It was possible.

I liked the way she looked. Her soft skin. Her sweet smile. Even her intense gaze as she studied a blueprint.

A look that usually led to a brilliant idea.

Beauty and brains. That's what Emma was.

The thought of her being deported had struck me in the heart.

I paced away from the bridal department. Watched the shoppers as they wandered the floors. A small family passed— the man pushing a baby cart... a woman walking beside him... one baby in the cart and another on the way.

That was the end game. The reason we worked so hard. To have the family of our own.

"Mr. Moore," Bree called from behind me.

I spun and walked back to the dressing room door.

"Emma will be right out," she said.

I glanced at my watch. Geez. How long did it take to try on a couple of dress? We had less than two hours to get this done, get to the appointment I'd made her at the salon, and get to Noah Worthington's house.

Having the wedding at Noah's, his wife had suggested, would lend legitimacy to the whole thing.

Then we had to send the paperwork to the immigration office, all before eight p.m.

Bree handed me a bottle of water.

"Sorry I don't have champagne," she said.

"It's okay." I didn't have time to relax with champagne anyway.

My phone chimed. Good. My tuxedo had been delivered to Noah's house. My measurements were on file with my tailor and I'd contacted him earlier to send over a black tux.

Bree held back the red curtain and at first all I could see was white.

Then Emma stepped out in the mermaid dress I'd picked out for her. Her brunette hair was down, swirling around her shoulders, framing her face.

Something burst in my heart. Like a bubble sending shards all through me.

But as the shards settled, I knew that this marriage was right.

And the dress?

Perfect.

13

EMMA

I stepped out from behind the curtain, feeling seriously ridiculous.

The vee-neck sleeveless form-fitting dress had a train that flowed around me from the waist down like a cloak.

Then I saw Harrison.

He was standing there with a bottle of water in one hand and his phone in the other.

His expression told me everything.

He approved.

"That's it," he said under his breath.

Bree was talking about how it needed a few tucks here and there, but neither one of us was listening to her.

Harrison motioned for me to turn.

Picking up the train, I slowly turned, watching him over my shoulder. After a brief pause, I turned the rest of the way and stopped.

"Get her some shoes," Harrison, his voice rough.

Bree asked my size and bustled off to get me shoes.

"What do you think?" I asked with a little smile.

Harrison seemed to pull himself together.

"It should serve the purpose," he said. "It fits you well."

"Bree says it needs to be adjusted."

"How does it feel?"

"Perfect," I said.

And now I'd gotten over feeling self-conscious, it really did feel perfect.

"Good," he said as Bree brought over some shoes.

As I sat on the sofa, Harrison stepped forward and exchanged his credit card for the shoes.

When he knelt in front of me, my heart rate skittered and my thoughts scattered.

I lifted my hem as he held one shoe for me, then the other.

Thank God I'd had my toes manicured two days ago. Sometimes I wondered why I bothered since no one ever saw my toes other than me.

But this one moment in time was worth all those times I'd endured sitting through a pedicure.

Still kneeling at my feet, he looked up at me, one arm over his knee.

"I feel like I should propose," he said.

My breath caught in my throat and I couldn't get any words out.

He was grinning at me now.

I took a deep breath and forced myself to focus.

But as inhaled deeply, I caught his ever so masculine scent. He smelled subtly woodsy and something I couldn't put a name to, but altogether it hit me in my core.

And all at once, I saw him in a different light. His short dark hair, brushing the collar of his white shirt. The familiar five o'clock shadow darkening his cheeks, giving him that dangerous edge that I'd tried to ignore these past months as we worked late together.

And those eyes. Those blue eyes with white shards shooting out. Shards that were only noticeable up close.

"You don't have to do that," I said, but I could barely hear my own voice."

He tilted his head to one side, that amused grin back on his face.

"Emma," he said.

I was shaking my head, though at what, I didn't know.

This man—Harrison—was my assistant. We worked together. We weren't dating.

But the way he was looking at me had every one of my cells on fire.

Everything around us faded. The fact that we were in Nordstrom's. That there were strangers around.

It occurred to me that we were doing everything backwards.

A man was supposed to propose before the girl bought the wedding dress.

How odd we must look to others.

"Emma," he said again. "Will you marry me?"

I wasn't supposed to feel this way. This was a business deal. Only.

But my stomach was full of butterflies.

I couldn't imagine that a real proposal could have felt any more magical than this moment.

In fact... if a man ever did propose to me—for real—this moment would overshadow it. I was certain of it.

I sucked in a breath. Acknowledged the moisture in my eyes.

"Yes," I said, unable to say anything else.

"Come here," he growled, pulling me onto his knee.

I gasped and put my arms around him, balancing on his knee, his arms around me.

Then the flash of a camera caught our attention.

14

HARRISON

*T*he magical moment of my proposal was dimmed by the flash of a camera.

I wasn't a famous man, by any means, nonetheless, the fact that our proposal had been captured on a stranger's phone sent a chill down my spine.

This proposal could be seen one of two ways. It could be seen as unbelievably magical. Or it could be seen as backwards and, thus, fishy.

But Bree clapped as she walked toward us.

"How romantic," she said, clasping her hands beneath her chin.

If Bree, who worked in a wedding department, found it romantic, then if that photo ever got out, it shouldn't do anything to blow our cover.

But despite all those thoughts that flew through my mind, they all paled as I looked at the faint blush on Emma's cheeks.

This marriage was supposed to be a sham... a business arrangement. So why did the proposal fee so real?

It was the heat of the moment, of course.

Then just as quickly as it started, it was over. Emma moved back to the sofa and Bree held out my credit card.

My phone chimed with a text. I took the credit card, put it back in my money clip, and checked my phone

SAVANNAH: *Hi Harrison. The salon is coming here. What is your ETA?*

I smiled at the message. Noah's wife always including a greeting with her text messages.

ME: *Leaving Nordstrom's now.*

"Ready to go?" I asked.

"I have to get changed," Emma said.

"We have to have the alterations done," Bree chimed in.

"What alterations?" I asked. "It fits perfectly."

"It's a little long," Bree said. "And a little loose around the waist."

"Bree," I said. "Thank you for your help. But honestly, no one will notice."

Another clerk came over with a shopping bag.

"I put your clothes in here," she told Emma with a smile. "Congratulations."

"Thank you," Emma said.

In that moment, this wedding was not a sham. In this moment, this wedding felt about as real as any wedding could.

I took the bag in one hand and Emma's hand with the other. Her hand felt delicate and small in mine. Just another one of the myriad things I did not know about the woman I was about to marry.

We'd have plenty of time to learn about each other.

That happy thought was chased by another. *It's not real. It's temporary.*

I ignored the smiles and well-wishes that greeted us as we made our way outside and waited for the car.

With her wearing yards and yards of silk, it took a minute to get her into the SUV.

Once she was inside, I jumped into the driver's seat and fastened my seat belt.

It was hard to say where we were going from here, but wherever it was, it felt like an adventure from where I was sitting.

And from the glow and little smile on Emma's face, I would put money on her feeling the same way.

15

EMMA

"We're having the wedding at Noah's house," Harrison said as he navigated the congested traffic around the Galleria.

"Noah?" I asked. "Noah Worthington?"

"Yes."

"How did that happen?"

How did we go from a sham wedding to avoid immigrations to a wedding at the boss's boss's house?

"I needed his help getting a judge onboard. The man can pull off anything."

"So he knows?" I asked, feeling sick.

"I had to tell him," Harrison said. "It was the only way I could make it happen. He's good though. He won't tell."

"You trust him?"

If Harrison trusted Noah, then I had no choice but to do so, also.

But still...

"Noah is a law-abiding citizen. If you told him what we're doing—which is illegal—then you're making him accessory."

"I trust him with my life."

Well hell.

I was already in too deep. The plane I was supposed to be boarding would be leaving in... I glanced at my watch. Less than one hour.

That option was no longer viable.

It was impossible to get to the airport from here in that short amount of time.

I'd gotten caught up in the heat of the moment. There was no other explanation.

I had to keep pulling myself back down to reality.

This was not a real wedding.

It was a business arrangement.

Harrison was kind, that was all.

Still. I couldn't explain away why it felt so real.

I wasn't one of those girls who had their wedding planned out by the time they were eleven-years-old. I hadn't dreamed in fairy tales. My life had always been based in reality, especially after I lost my parents.

After that happened, any fancifulness I might have had left from being a young child had been jerked away.

And the world had become a dangerous place.

And yet here I was. Being fanciful with my head in the clouds.

I stared out the window at the passing shops. Harrison turned and, staying off the freeways, drove through the subdivisions. So many apartment buildings of all shapes and sizes. I made a mental note of some of the names of the complexes so I could look them up online. Look at their floor plans.

Obviously, I was easily distracted.

I looked back over at Harrison when we stopped at a stoplight.

He was scowling at his phone.

"What?" I asked.

"Our charade is starting sooner than we thought."

16

EMMA

*W*e pulled into Noah and Savannah Worthington's circle drive and pulled off the side onto the stone driveway leading to the closed garage and parked.

They could accommodate a lot of vehicles and Harrison obviously knew where to park.

I was too tense to say anything.

Noah's daughter Wynter was showing up to video our wedding and as far as she knew it was a real wedding.

They were calling it a surprise wedding. It was a surprise alright.

How we ended up at Noah's house, I couldn't say. I did know that the Worthingtons were known for pulling employees under their wing.

Harrison came around and opened my door.

He leaned against it and held out his hand.

When I put my hand in his, instead of pulling me out of the car, he held my hand until our eyes met.

He was so handsome.

"Don't be nervous, love," he said.

He smiled at my now doubt shocked expression.

"We can do this," he said. "Just pretend you're in love with me."

My heart tripped at his words and there was something in his eyes that made me think he was far too good at this *pretending*.

Deep down, I wasn't so sure just how much pretending I was going to have to do.

Then as though he'd said nothing out of the ordinary...

Just pretend to be in love with the guy was merely your assistant —not your boyfriend—only hours ago.

He steadied me as I got myself and the mermaid dress with its yards of train cloaked around it, out of the car.

It occurred to me, as I walked toward the front door of Noah Worthington's two-story manor, that I was sorely overdressed. Harrison, the groom, was wearing slacks and a long sleeve-white button-down shirt. Casual Friday attire.

"I'm overdressed," I said. One hand was tucked in the crook of his arm, the other holding up the hem of the dress.

"You're the bride," he said. "Not possible for you to be overdressed."

I glanced down at his casual clothes.

He just smiled that little secret smile.

"Not for long," he said.

I said nothing in response. My attention was focused now on walking up the stone stairs leading to the front door.

As we walked across an immaculate veranda, the door opened and a middle-age woman, formally dressed in black with a white apron answered the door.

"Come in, Harrison," she said. "and Miss Bailey. It's a pleasure to meet you."

"Thank you, Mary," Harrison said, as we stepping into the foyer.

The house looked like it could have been a showcase in

Southern Home magazine. Vases on the occasional tables held fresh white and pink daisies.

"I'll show Miss Bailey to the downstairs guest room," she said. "You can head upstairs."

Harrison turned to me, holding both my hands in his, and leaned forward.

"You look beautiful, my love," he said, his soft words giving me chills. "I'll see you shortly."

I nodded. Reminded myself that we were pretending to be so madly in love that we were having a surprise wedding.

"Come on," Mary said. "Everyone's waiting on you."

"Everyone?" I looked questioningly at Harrison.

He just shrugged and released my hand.

Then he kissed me lightly on the cheek.

"Enjoy," he whispered against my ear.

17

HARRISON

I watched Emma as she went, however reluctantly, with Mary to the left toward the hallway leading to the guest room.

Even from here, I could hear female voices drifting along the hallway. That would be a hair stylist, a make-up person, and my stepsister Wynter.

Emma had no idea what she was in for. I sincerely hoped that she could relax enough to enjoy it. Sham or not, this was a real wedding. The Worthingtons were pulling out all the stops.

There would be no doubt from looking at the photos that it was real.

As I jogged up the stairs toward one of the other guest rooms, I felt a twinge of regret.

Not regret about marrying Emma. On the contrary. I felt a twinge of regret that it wasn't for real.

As promised, my tuxedo waited for me. Someone had left it lying on the bed in a garment bag. I stepped into the shower, then took my time getting dressed.

The clock was ticking, but I had far less to do than Emma.

Clean-shaven and dressed, I looked the part of a groom.

It wasn't a hardship being with Emma... pretending to be in love with her.

It was funny, though, because this morning I never saw this coming.

If anyone had asked me this time yesterday if I would be getting married today, to my boss, I would have laughed.

But now I wasn't laughing.

I did, however, have a goofy grin on my face.

Running a hand over my chin, I tried to wipe it off, but it did no good.

I'm just playing a part. I told myself that anyway.

Maybe enjoying playing my part a little too much, but playing my part, nonetheless.

There were about a hundred details to figure out from here.

Things that most real couples spent months figuring out.

We had hours.

Whatever we did, we'd claim it as spontaneity. Lover's spontaneity.

I had little doubt that we could make it look real. Although I'd never thought of Emma that way, now that I had, I couldn't get her out of my head.

After buttoning my shirt and putting on the matching vest, I tied the wide tie and tucked it into the vest.

I stood in front of the full-length mirror and examined the look. Except for the white shirt, everything else—pants, jacket, vest, tie—was a deep silver. I was pleased with the very classic look my tailor had chosen.

My hands trembled a bit and I stuck them in my pockets.

I turned when Noah knocked on the door.

"Come in," I said.

Noah stood there, dressed in a charcoal tux, himself, looking quite dapper for a semi-retired man.

Insurance only allowed Noah to fly local flights. Arbitrary

age limitations. Everyone knew he could outpilot any one of the people hired to fly for Skye Travels.

He walked over to the minibar and took out two glasses.

"Whiskey?" he asked.

"Sure," I said. Maybe it would help to steady my nerves.

He poured a splash of amber liquid into two shot glasses and handed me one.

He held up his glass for a toast.

"To doing the right thing," he said and I tipped my glass against his.

We tipped our glasses back and drank. The warm liquid burned all the way down to my stomach.

Mission accomplished. I was sufficiently distracted, at least for the moment.

"You sure about this?" Noah asked leaning against the bed post.

A valid question.

One I didn't expect very many people to understand. My mother for one.

My mother, Claire Beauchamp had married Noah as part of a business arrangement designed by their fathers. But after their divorce, she had bumped into her old sweetheart and just like that, she was a hopeless romantic again.

Nonetheless, I knew what I was doing.

"Yes," I said. "I'm sure."

"It's no small thing you're doing."

"Yes sir. I know."

"You think it might grow into something more?"

Maybe I needed another shot of whiskey.

Noah had just cut to the quick of the whole thing.

Did I think it could turn into something more?

Hadn't I just been wishing that it was real?

Didn't I have her in my head? My thoughts?

Seeing her in that wedding dress with her hair down had tripped something in my heart.

Something that must have been simmering below the surface for quite some time and I hadn't even been aware of it.

"Anything's possible," I said.

Noah just grinned. "She's a looker."

My thoughts exactly.

18

EMMA

I closed my eyes and tried to do exactly what Harrison had suggested; however, it was easier said than done.

The Worthingtons had a bathroom that was set up perfectly for doing a girl's hair and makeup.

A girl named Rosie had washed my hair and was drying it straight and smooth with a hot blow dryer and a round brush. Another girl, named Ethel, did my makeup. It was surreal sitting beneath the cape, being pampered and transformed into a lovely bride. The two girls chattered to themselves, leaving me to my own thoughts.

Everything about the day seemed to be going backwards. I was already wearing the dress. Normally a girl would have her hair dried before getting into her wedding gown. Right?

Not that I was an expert on being a bride getting ready for her wedding.

Rosie and Ethel believed that my wedding was real.

"Girl," Ethel said. "You must be over the moon. I saw your man when y'all came in. Handsome."

I smiled, not even trying to talk over the roar of the hair dryer.

Ethel applied a touch of blush to my cheeks as Rosie switched off the hair dryer.

"Up or down?" she asked Ethel.

"Definitely down," Ethel said.

"Agreed."

Rosie lightly brushed my hair and sprayed it with something that smelled like daffodils in springtime.

Then she whirled me around to face the mirror.

I sucked in my breath. Somehow these two women had transformed me into a princess.

For the second time today, I had the feeling that if I ever got married for real, the day would be overshadowed by this one.

I felt like I'd stepped into a fairy tale world.

I took a deep breath as I stood in front of the full-length mirror and ran a hand along my flat stomach.

This was it. This was my wedding day.

Real or not, this was it. I was ruined for any other wedding day.

A young lady with a camera stepped up behind me and started taking pictures.

Holding the camera in her left hand, she held out her right hand.

"Hi," she said. "I'm Wynter. Noah's daughter. Is it okay with you if I take some pictures?"

Wynter was a beautiful young lady, maybe late twenties, wearing a tasteful white sheath dress with a sweetheart neckline and long sleeves.

She smiled with perfect bow-shaped lips, making me feel immediately relaxed.

"Sure," I said, shaking her hand.

"Welcome to the family."

I'd heard that the Worthingtons tended to take their employees into their fold and make them feel like family.

My eyes misted over, but I fought back the tears.

I had no family of my own.

It was just me against the world.

But I couldn't—wouldn't—cry. It wouldn't do to ruin my makeup.

"Come on," Wynter said. "Let's have a glass of champagne."

19

HARRISON

I froze as I walked next to Noah toward the stairs. Wedding music drifted from downstairs.

"You don't like the music?" Noah asked.

I shook my head. "The music is great. It's not that. I forgot something."

"What's that?" Noah asked.

"Rings. Can't have a wedding without rings."

Noah grinned. "I didn't forget. They're downstairs."

I stepped forward again. "You thought of everything."

"You have Savannah to thank for that one," he said.

"I don't know how I'll ever repay you two for this."

"Just give it a chance to work."

I shot him a glance as we started down the stairs.

"I know the reason behind what you're doing," Noah said. "But I've seen strong marriages start off with less than a friendship."

"Friendship?" Maybe his shit was slipping. "You know I'm her assistant, right?"

Noah clapped me on the back. "Assistant or not, only a friend would do what you're doing."

"It's nothing really," I said, vocalizing what I kept telling myself, as we reached the bottom of the stairs.

Noah just nodded and we went into the formal parlor.

It was a large, tastefully furnished room. A gas fireplace that looked like a real wood burning fireplace. An oversized sofa. Long dark blue velvet drapes framing the floor to ceiling windows.

A steel blue wool rug covered the area between the sofa and the fireplace.

Judge Benson, an older man, was already there, standing on one side of the fireplace.

"Judge Benson," Noah said. "this is Harrison."

"It's a pleasure to meet you," Judge Benson said, holding out his hand.

"You too," I said. "It's very kind of you to do this at the last minute."

"Ah. Noah and I go way back. He's come to my rescue more times than I count. It's the least I can do."

Noah walked over to the mantle and picked up a light blue box.

"I'll let you do the honors," he said.

I opened the box—Tiffany's—to reveal a perfect solitaire diamond ring.

"Savannah always goes for the classic look," Noah said.

"I couldn't have done better myself."

Noah beamed. He'd been married to his wife Savannah for years, long enough to have five children together, now married adults, but he still had unparalleled pride for his wife.

I looked from the rings to Noah and Judge Benson.

Somehow my fake wedding had gone from simply helping my boss to having all the trappings of a real wedding. Including my Godparents, a judge, and Tiffany rings.

The only thing that would have made it more real would

have been for us to have a houseful of people including my family.

I wondered if I could avoid telling my mother about the wedding.

It would probably look a bit suspicious if anyone came investigating.

No. I would have to tell my parents.

Knowing that did what nothing else could to remind me of the gravity of what I was doing.

I put an arm on the mantle to steady myself.

Noah looked at his phone.

"I have you a flight scheduled for the morning."

"For what?" Was he sending me home? To tell my parents already?

"Your honeymoon. To Mackinac Island."

20

EMMA

"How long have you known Harrison?" Wynter asked, pouring two glasses of champagne.

"About four months," I said. I didn't know much about these kinds of things, but I knew that sticking as close to the truth as possible was for the best.

"Really? That's quick." She handed me a flute of champagne.

If she thought four months was quick, she had no idea.

The bubbles tickled my lips as I tasted the champagne.

"When did he propose?"

Oh no. Harrison and I hadn't planned for these kinds of questions. He could be saying one thing while I was saying another.

I set the little flute on the table next to me.

We sat in a little sitting room with a wonderful view of the well-lit back patio.

"Today," I said. "We didn't want to wait," I added in response to her shocked expression.

She smiled. "That is so romantic."

"Quinn and I didn't want to wait either." She shrugged. "But it was the second time around for us."

"How so?" I asked, relieved to get the conversation off me.

"We met in college. But I disappeared into the Air Force for ten years. Then my father, of all things, offered me a job. And... well... Quinn just happened to be there."

"Ten years and you just accidentally found each other?"

"Yes. And then I disappeared again, but he tracked me down in Boston. The rest is history, as they say."

"I've heard that Skye Travels is magical like that."

"Yes," she said, putting a hand on my arm. "It is magical like that." She lowered her voice. "They say it started with my father accidentally finding Momma again after twenty years."

"It's so wonderful that you have stories like that."

"What about you? What about your family?"

I shook my head. "I don't have any family."

"Oh. I'm so sorry."

"Don't be." I picked up my champagne and took a quick gulp. "No need to apologize. I've been on my own for a really long time."

"At least now you have Harrison."

I blinked. Yes. Now I had Harrison.

But was having Harrison opening a whole Pandora's box?

Wedding music drifted down the hallway.

"I think they're calling us," she said. "Are you ready?"

I took a deep breath. How could I possibly be ready?

I was about to marry a complete stranger.

"Yes," I said. "I'm ready."

21

HARRISON

*W*e waited in the parlor. Noah had the rings in his pocket. Savannah sat on the sofa. Wynter was somewhere with Emma.

A harpist sat in the far corner, playing soft romantic music.

Noah, standing next to me, put a hand on my shoulder.

"Are you good?" he asked.

I nodded. "I am. It feels so real."

"It is real, Son," Noah said. "It's as real as you make it."

I straightened and put my hands behind my back.

As real as I made it.

Whatever that meant.

"Do you mind if I walk her down the aisle?"

"That would be kind of you," I said.

Noah disappeared and a few minutes later, the wedding march started.

Wynter came to the door, smiled, and came forward to stand nearby.

Then the music changed and Noah appeared at the door.

Then Emma.

My breath caught in my throat.

Oh. My. God.

Emma was breathtakingly stunning.

Someone had thought to get her a bouquet of flowers.

Noah and Savannah had taken care of so many details on a moment's notice. They were truly amazing.

Emma scanned the room, gaze coming to land on mine.

The little smile that spread across her lips brightened her whole face.

I felt like I'd been socked in the gut.

It's as real as you make it.

Her arm on Noah's, she walked toward me.

Judge Benson stood next to me, waiting patiently.

This wedding was real.

I let go of any remaining thoughts about it being fake. Let those thoughts just dissolve.

Then she was standing next to me.

She handed her bouquet to Wynter and I took both her hands in mine.

Her green eyes sparkled like morning dew.

There were so many things I knew about this woman. More than I'd known about any of the women I'd ever dated.

I knew that she like lattes in the morning, extra vanilla. I knew that the reason she avoided small talk was because she was nervous around people. I knew that she didn't like cold weather, but she liked thunderstorms.

The only time I'd ever seen her stop working to stare outside was during thunderstorms.

"Who presents this woman to be married to this man?"

"I do," Noah said, then went to sit next to his wife on the sofa. Their automatically clasped together, even after all these years together.

That's what I wanted.

But now my attention was focused entirely on Emma.

Judge Benson was talking, but I didn't hear a word he was saying.

All I knew was that I wanted to love, honor, and cherish this woman for the rest of my days.

22

EMMA

"I do." The words slipped so easily, so naturally from my lips.

Harrison's hands held mine tightly, our eyes locked.

He smelled like cedar and sandalwood and something else totally masculine. I wanted to burrow myself against him and never let go.

He was so handsome in his dark pewter tuxedo and white shirt.

I lost myself in him, letting the rest of the world fade away.

Then he took my hand and slipped a ring onto my left hand. Two rings. A diamond solitaire and a plain wedding band.

Was this mine? Or was this a prop? It had to be real.

Then someone pressed a ring into my hand and, my hands trembling, I slipped it on Harrison's finger.

Judge Benson was saying something, but his words didn't register.

Then he stopped talking for a moment. A moment of silence.

Harrison and I both turned and looked at him. I blinked.

Judge Benson smiled.

"You may now kiss the bride."

With a silent gasp, I turned back to Harrison.

He was smiling at me.

How had I not prepared myself for this moment? I'd totally gapped on this.

Harrison pulled me close, into his arms.

He pressed his lips against the corner of mine. Just the corner, but my whole body ignited.

Harrison pulled back enough to look into my eyes... searching... then he put both his hands on my cheeks and pressed his lips against mine.

I melted against him.

He felt so good. So right.

Then the music started again and Harrison pulled away.

I was left yearning for more.

"I now pronounce you husband and wife."

A round of applause followed when we turned and Harrison held up our clasped hands.

Wynter hugged me, then Savannah.

Everyone hugged Harrison.

Noah took my free hand and kissed me on the cheek.

"Welcome to the family," he said, for my ears only.

That was twice today someone had said that to me.

And, again, I didn't understand it, but I accepted it.

These people had put on a wedding for us that rivaled many "real" weddings.

No, I thought, they put on a real wedding for us.

The woman, Jan, came in carrying a wedding cake.

"It was the best I could find on short notice," she said, apologetically.

"It's beautiful," I murmured.

The solid white cake was in the design of a castle with the

shape of a fairy tale carriage replete with a horse made into the front of it.

Jan beamed. "I have a friend," she said.

With this cake. With Harrison holding my hand, I felt like I had truly stepped into the pages of a fairy tale.

23

HARRISON

I sat next to Emma, one arms around her, on the sofa in Noah and Savannah's parlor.

Judge Benson stood talking with Noah.

Savannah and Wynter stood next to the cake, Wynter taking pictures.

I held both of Emma's hands, keeping her pressed against me.

However we had gotten here didn't matter at this point.

She felt so right. So perfect.

I never wanted to let go of her.

"Are you okay?" I asked, pressing my cheek against hers.

Her face was slightly flushed, her lips parted.

"Yes," she said. "That was beautiful... so real."

"It was real," I said, echoing Noah's words. "As real as we want it to be."

She looked up at me sharply.

"What do you mean?" Her voice was barely a whisper.

I kissed her on the cheek.

Was it too soon to tell her that I wanted to be married to her for real?

I knew it was, as much as I didn't want it to be.

She needed time to settle. Time to become accustomed to the idea of being married to me.

It wasn't normal to wake up in the morning, single, no boyfriend, to being married at the end of the day. Married to your assistant. Maybe if we'd been friends...

Although we spent all day, most every day together, I hadn't thought of Emma as a friend.

She had, in fact, annoyed me in so many ways.

But now those things that annoyed me, no longer did.

"Come and cut the cake," Wynter said, holding up a knife.

"Shall we?" I asked Emma.

"Okay."

I unwrapped myself from her and stood up. Then I took both her hands and pulled her up with me.

Keeping her close, we walked to the cake and Wynter handed her the knife.

"It's too pretty to cut," she said.

"I'll help you," I said, putting my hand over hers.

We slid the knife through the castle wall and the back of the carriage.

Wynter was there with plates.

Since this was a very informal reception, we took the first two pieces and took our seats again.

I put a bite of cake on a fork and held it while she took it into her mouth.

"This is really good," she said.

"What?" Wedding cake isn't supposed to taste good."

"I know. Right?"

She picked her own fork while I tasted it.

"You're right," I said. "It is good."

She smiled up at me and I knew I was in trouble.

I was falling in love with my fake wife.

24

EMMA

*A*lone for the first time since I received the news that I was being deported, I stood alone in one of Noah Worthington's upstairs guest bedrooms.

Since Noah and Savannah Worthington had raised five children, they had plenty of bedrooms to convert into guest rooms.

This particular room had a large four-poster bed with a white comforter and matching pillow shams. The only furniture was an armchair and a little writing desk with a lamp. There was a gas fireplace on one side and French windows that led out onto a balcony on another.

The room was as big as the whole second floor of my two-bedroom condo.

I wondered what it must have been like to grow up in a room like this. I couldn't even fathom it. I tried to imagine posters of heartthrobs on the walls. A bright pink bean bag chair. Pink throw pillows. Barbie dolls strewn around the room.

But that had been my room. This room, at some point, had belonged to a child from a different world.

I sat on the bed and first time in hours checked my phone. It was just after eleven o'clock. Nearly midnight.

I couldn't remember the last time I'd stayed up this late. College maybe.

No messages.

It was my wedding day and I had no messages.

Over the years, I'd kept my distance from people. It was safer that way. I'd had a few boyfriends along the way, but nothing worth keeping.

Nothing like Harrison.

I lay back on the bed, kicked off my heels, and looked at the ceiling.

The wedding had been magical. I'd seen Noah Worthington around the building, but I'd never been introduced to him.

He was a legend around Worthington Enterprises. The original founder of Skye Travels—the company that had started everything.

And he'd walked me down the aisle.

Then when I'd stood there in front of that judge with Harrison, the rest of the world had faded away.

There had been no one in the world but us.

Then when he'd kissed me, my world had tilted on its axis.

When his lips had touched mine, I'd known right then that my world was never going to be the same again.

It was a fake wedding. Until it wasn't.

Sitting up, I reached behind me. There was no way I was going to get these buttons undone.

I seriously considered sleeping in my wedding gown, but that was simply insane.

Harrison was in the room next door.

I'd just go over there, get him to unbutton the dress, and come back to this heavenly soft bed for sleep.

I gathered up my skirts so as not to step on the hem and tiptoed across the room to the door.

I slowly opened the door and stepped out into the darkened hallway.

Staying close to the wall, I moved down to where I knew Harrison was sleeping.

Holding my breath, I knocked on his door.

I waited as the seconds ticked past.

My only plan B was to sleep in the dress.

I was just about to go back to my own room when the door opened.

Harrison stood there, grinning at me.

"It's my wife," he said, sweeping a hand to invite me inside. "Come in."

"I just—"

"Don't be silly," he said. "Come in. You'll blow our cover."

He'd taken off his jacket and tie and one corner of his white shirt hung loose.

He looked... relaxed.

I stepped inside and he closed the door.

"Let me guess," he said, peering at me. "You need help with your buttons."

"How did you know?" I asked.

He just grinned. "I have sisters."

"Right." I turned my back to him and shoved my hair to the side. "If you could just..."

"Come," he said. "I want to show you something."

"Seriously?"

Didn't he know how late it was? But I followed him out on the balcony, a balcony which connected to my room. I hadn't had to go through the hallway after all.

"Look," he said, pointing up at the bright full moon, hanging low in the sky.

"It's beautiful," I said, going to the railing as though I could see better from there.

White wispy clouds drifted by, but the moon stood steady.

"It's a beautiful way to end such a lovely day," he said.

I leaned against the railing and kicked my right foot back.

"It was a beautiful wedding."

"Agreed. Noah and Savannah really came through."

"It's amazing how they managed that."

"They're amazing."

I looked over my shoulder at him. He was standing next to me now.

"Do they do this kind of thing for everyone?"

"Of course not..." he said. "I've known them a long time. They're awesome."

"I've never met anyone like them," I mused. "To just take employees under their wing like that."

"That could be how they got to be so successful."

There were certainly a lot of things that went into building something so successful as Worthington Enterprises, but customer loyalty was no doubt a big part of it.

And they had mine.

25

HARRISON

The glistening moonlight, smelling of dewy daffodils, spilled over Emma's sleek raven hair.

She turned her face up toward the moonlight and closed her eyes.

She stood there, like a siren beckoning me toward the dangerous rocks.

Although she'd come to me asking for help unbuttoning her dress, there were two very valid reasons why I would put that off as long as possible.

The first was that once I obliged her, she would leave and return to her room.

The second, more dangerous reason, was that once I got my hands near her skin, I would be unable to resist pulling her close and making her a bride in every sense.

But she trusted me, my innocent Emma. As she should.

It was my job to protect her and take care of her—even if it meant to protect her from myself.

I'd kissed her, but it had been part of the show. Part of the sham.

Okay, maybe I'd kissed her with more enthusiasm than was required for our sham wedding.

And, for me, the kiss had been more than just part of the ceremony.

The kiss had been real.

And it wasn't enough. It would never be enough. She was like a drug that I couldn't get enough of.

We were legally married. Bound by paperwork. And to avoid going to prison we had to make it look real to everyone we encountered.

We were doing a good job of that so far.

Hell, I was convinced the marriage was real.

But not my shy architect.

She was by the book. The fact that she had agreed to marry me to begin with spoke to the level of her commitment to staying in the states.

When she turned and smiled at me, I turned inside out.

I'd worked closely with her for four months, scheduling all her appointments, making sure she remembered to eat on those days when she got so wrapped up in her work that she forgot, and learning tricks of design and negotiation from her.

I'd known exactly where she was for four months and I'd learned to anticipate her needs before she did.

Right now my brain was clouded with thoughts of pulling her close and kissing her again.

I wasn't in tune with her needs right now.

Unless, she was begging me to kiss her again.

Surely I was just imagining that.

It was the moonlight. The moonlight and haze of the day.

The wedding had been truly magical.

Like a fairy tale.

I was supposed to be the logical one. She was the creative one.

But the way she was smiling at me took everything I knew and turned it upside down.

"Is this what you wanted to show me?" she asked.

"What?" I shook myself. "Yes. Would you like a glass of champagne?"

So much for being hip, slick, and cool.

26

EMMA

*H*arrison held the door for me as we went back inside his room.

He went to the bar, took out two glasses, and a bottle of champagne waiting in a bucket of ice.

Someone had obviously thought that we'd be needing champagne for the night.

He popped the cork and after filling two glass, handed one to me.

I sat on the one armchair in the room.

Harrison held up a glass.

"To us," he said.

I held up my glass to his, the glasses clinking together in a toast.

We both sipped the sweet bubbly wine, then he sat on the arm chair next to me.

"We have a lot to do, don't we?" I asked, mostly to distract myself from how close he was.

He blew out a breath. "You can say that again."

I twirled the glass stem between my hands. "You really want me to move into your condo?"

He nodded. "Yes."

"And what do I do with mine?"

"Sell it?"

I could sell it. Getting out from under the mortgage wouldn't be a bad thing.

"So… I'd pay rent? To you?"

He shook his head.

"You worry too much."

"I want to pull my weight." I tilted my head so I could look up at him.

"My place is paid for. There's no need to worry."

I nodded slowly.

For a recent grad, he was in a good position. But then he'd taken some time before college. Obviously did something to make some money. Get himself established before going to school. There was plenty of time to find all that out.

But I'd give him his privacy. The most he told me about himself, the more I'd have to disclose about me. So I wouldn't press him for information.

But did I want to do that? Did I want to start over again after two years?

I didn't have a crystal ball. Two years was a really long time.

In the event that I did end up being deported, I would at least have my property taken care of.

It wasn't the worst idea.

"You don't have to decide about that right now," he said.

"I know."

Then he slid to the floor on one knee and took my hands in his.

I flashed back to that moment in Nordstrom's when he'd proposed to me.

And my heart responded in much the same way it had then.

"Emma," he said. "I'm going to take care of you. You have to trust me."

"But why?" I asked. "You don't know me."

"I know you as well as I know anyone."

He had a good point.

We probably did know each other as well as a lot of people who actually got married—for real.

We could have this conversation all day long. Going back and forth, but it wasn't going to change anything. I didn't even know what it was I wanted him to say. He'd said and done everything right. More than anyone in his shoes could be expected to do.

The problem was mine. I couldn't get enough of him... and I didn't know what to do about it.

My heart was pounding so fast, I was certain he could hear my blood pounding.

"Alright," I said. "I should get some sleep. Before this champagne goes to my head."

But I didn't move. And he didn't move.

27

HARRISON

*E*mma's breath was coming shallow. I could see it in the way her chest moved beneath the sweetheart neckline. She needed to go. To get some sleep. But she didn't move.

Of course, she couldn't move since I was blocking her way.

"Good idea," I said. A very unfair remark since I did nothing to assist her in this move.

Tilting her head to one side, she looked at me.

I just grinned.

After a moment, she sat back against the chair and appeared to relax. Appeared being the optimal word. I could tell by the way she held her head to one side that she was anything but relaxed. She was purposely appearing to be relaxed.

Like she did when she was negotiating with a client— waiting for them to come around to her way of thinking.

I sat back on my heels.

Despite my reluctance to let her go, the gentleman in me won out.

If she'd been anyone else, I'm not sure what I would have done. But she was her.

In one swift motion, I stood up and held out a hand.

I caught the quick look of confusion that crossed her features... or was it disappointment? Either way, she put her hands in mine and allowed me to help her to her feet.

It was only then that I noticed she was barefoot.

I noticed because as I pulled her close to me, she was several inches shorter than she had been before.

Why that struck me as being so incredibly sexy, I couldn't say.

I shifted, putting one hand at the small of her back, my hand against the soft silk of her dress while I laced the fingers of my other hand with hers.

The movement brought her chin up and her gaze touched mine.

This was not a good idea.

I groaned and placed my lips gently against her.

She leaned in, wrapping one arm around my waist, the other around my neck.

So soft... so pliant.

I pulled her closer until her softness was pressed against my firm chest.

My tongue ran along the edges of her lips, taking in the perfect outline. Then I gently sucked her bottom lip and a soft moan drifted from her.

My resolve faltered as she leaned against me and her lips opened.

Unable to resist, my tongue slid inside her mouth and I tasted her. So sweet. I wanted to eat her up. I couldn't get enough.

My hands tangled in her hair, mussing it up.

I lifted her off the ground and sat down with her in my lap.

A lapful of soft woman and soft silk.

I put my hands on the sides of her face and she looked at me with hooded eyes. Those beautiful sparkling green eyes.

"You're beautiful," I whispered.

Her eyes drifted closed again and our lips were back together again.

If I spent the rest of my life kissing her just like this, I could die a happy man.

28

EMMA

I was drunk on Harrison's kisses.

This man I had willingly and happily married.

It occurred to me in the deep recesses of my mind that the remarkable moments of my life were marked by sudden, unexpected change.

My parents had died suddenly, sending me to live with my grandmother. That had led to the first time I'd changed my course. Her father, my great-grandfather had been from America. A World War II veteran who'd died in Germany.

I'd spent those three years looking at photos Grandma kept on the walls of her husband and father.

Granny also had me watching old movies set during WWII. And the time had become part of my psyche.

That's when I decided to go to college in America.

A sudden event that changed my life.

I'd chosen my major on a less traumatic, but equally sudden and random event.

It was my sophomore year. When I went in to register for my classes, the business class I needed was full so I had about half a minute to choose an elective.

An architectural class was available, so I'd signed up for it. It had been love at first sight.

That afternoon I'd changed my major to architecture.

Then there was today and my wedding with Harrison.

With the imminent threat of deportation or prison, I had been offered a marriage to Harrison.

A half minute to decide and I had chosen him.

Unbeknownst to me, marrying my assistant was a life altering event in more ways than one.

Not just avoiding being deported, but this kiss... this kiss was life-altering.

Even if nothing came of it in the long run with Harrison, I was changed.

This marriage, no matter how it had come about, was indelibly real on my psyche. Just like my great-grandfather from America.

Harrison kissed my cheeks, my eyelids, then back to my lips.

"So beautiful," he said, running his hands through my hair.

Putting his lips back on mine.

I couldn't get enough of him... get close enough to him.

He felt so right.

His lips traveled across my cheeks, to my ears, sending uncontrollable shivers through me.

He held my face close between his hands, planted little kisses on every inch of my cheeks, my eyelids, my lips.

"Emma," he said.

"Yes?" I said, barely able to catch my breath.

"I love you."

"What?"

His words jarred me out of the haziness of my thoughts.

"No," I said, pulling away.

This was supposed to be temporary. Fake. Not real.

It had an expiration date on it. Letting myself believe that it was could be more—was more—would be too painful.

When the two years were up and it was time to get divorced, I would be the one left holding the broken heart.

29

HARRISON

*A*s much as it hurt me, I had to let her go.

Her bare feet pattered against the wood floor as she left my room and went down the hallway to her own room. Her door clicked closed.

I stood there, in the middle of my room, staring out the open door into the darkened hallway.

I'd gotten carried away in the moment. Everything I was feeling was real.

Somewhere along the way, the pretending had stopped, for me, at least.

Nordstrom's was the first time I'd noticed that I wasn't pretending anymore. When I'd gotten on my knees and proposed to her, I had been sincere.

When I'd said *I do*, I had been sincere.

When I'd kissed her, I had been sincere.

And when I'd said I loved her, I had meant it.

The words had come from my heart.

But they had sent her running from me.

I picked up my champagne flute and drained the glass.

I paced to the window… to the door… and back again.

She'd come here to ask me to unbutton her dress. That was all.

She hadn't come here for me to kiss her.

And now she was in her room again, still wearing her wedding dress.

I filled the champagne flute again, watching the bubbles, but I didn't drink.

Instead I went to the window, leaned against it, and tried to regain some semblance of rational thought.

I'd married Emma with the agreement that we would have a marriage in name only. That we would pretend to be married to everyone we encountered so that we could convince immigrations that the marriage was actually real. That we could pass any investigation into the legitimacy of the marriage.

But it had become real. And along with that, I had begun to treat her like a real bride.

It was raining now. The raindrops splashed against the window panes. Thunder crashed in the distance. It was going to storm.

I'd fallen in love with Emma.

The fall had been fast and hard.

I'd known her as a boss. As someone I was paid to take care of.

Although she had annoyed me at times, I'd somehow started to care for her.

And then things had moved from there.

I should probably just lie down. Get some sleep.

Given her the evening and start again in the morning.

But I wasn't always known for doing what I was supposed to do.

I paced back across the room and stopped at the door.

I was standing at one of those crossroads.

The next few minutes could alter the direction of our relationships.

I had to choose wisely.

30

EMMA

I dropped onto the bed and laid back, fisting my hands in the downy white comforter.

My heart was pounding far too fast.

Putting a hand over my eyes, I forced myself to take deep breaths, but it didn't do much in the way of calming me.

I could still feel Harrison's lips against mine.

I could still be there with him, but I'd dashed off liked he'd said something offensive.

I was just tired. That had to be it. It had been a long, emotional day.

When was the last time a man had professed to be in love with me?

There was a guy in college. What was his name? Christopher something.

We'd broken up shortly after that. Actually I'd broken up with him. I couldn't even remember why. Not that it mattered. We'd been too different. On two different paths.

I could just sleep in the dress. I was so tired, I didn't care.

Then something was pecking at the window.

I gasped and sat straight up, putting my bare feet on the cool wood floor.

"Emma?"

Harrison?

I went to the window and carefully peaked behind the curtain.

Harrison was standing there at my French door.

I ran a hand over the wood, finding the lock in the darkness and flipping it.

The door opened and I was face to face with Harrison.

"I'm sorry," he said.

"No." I shook my head. "You shouldn't be sorry." My breath caught in my throat.

"Turn around," he said.

"What?"

"Just turn around."

I turned my back to him. He gently swept my hair to one side and began to slowly and methodically unbutton the buttons on my gown.

I took a deep breath and blew it out.

"Thank you," I said, over my shoulder.

"My pleasure."

When he made his way to my waist and unbuttoned the last one, he stopped and rested his hands around my waist.

I didn't move.

Then he leaned forward and I could feel his breath against my cheek. My eyes fluttered closed.

"Good night, my love," he whispered.

I took a moment for me to realize that he'd released me.

Opening my eyes, I turned around, but he was gone.

Nothing but moonlight met my gaze.

"Good night," I whispered.

My hands trembled as I closed the door and clicked the lock back into place.

The dress slipped from my shoulders and I stepped out of it.

With a sigh, I tossed the dress on the back of the armchair, then climbed into the bed.

31

HARRISON

I woke early the next morning with a text from Noah. Noelle Worthington, one of the Skye Travels pilots, was going to be flying Emma and me to Mackinac Island on one of the company's private jets. Our flight was scheduled for ten o'clock. A decent time to leave. We'd have a late lunch at the Grand Hotel.

I showered and dressed, feeling at a definite advantage. I had extra clothes here, but Emma didn't.

As her assistant, I hadn't done a very good job of taking care of that particular detail. I should have sent for some of her clothes last night.

But I had been quite caught up in everything. The wedding… Kissing Emma… Falling in love with her…

That's what I would do this morning.

Grabbing my money clip and phone, I headed downstairs.

No one was around. Noah and Savannah were already gone to their respective offices.

I followed the scent of French toast to the kitchen.

"Good morning," Jan said, looking over her shoulder.

"Good morning," I said. "Smells wonderful."

"Just some French toast. Planning to make a big breakfast for the happy couple. Let me know when you're ready. Eggs. Hashbrowns. Bacon. You name it."

"French toast is fine," I said, sliding onto one of the bar stool at the kitchen island.

"Coming right up," Jan said, flipping the pancake in the skillet. "It was a beautiful wedding."

"It was, wasn't it? Noah and Savannah are miracle workers."

"My niece is thinking about doing a surprise wedding."

"Surprise?"

"Yeah. Like you did. It's trending now, you know. Just invite some people over and... surprise! It's a wedding."

I laughed.

"Didn't know that's what they called it."

"It's alright," Jan flipped the pancake into a plate, added some butter, and set it front of me.

I picked up the syrup and doused it with a very politically incorrect amount of syrup.

"You make the best pancakes," I said.

Jan beamed. She really was the best cook and the Worthingtons were lucky to have her.

"Don't tell Emma," I said.

"Your secret is mine."

I took another bite. Noticed Jan was cleaning up.

"Would you make me another?"

"Of course," she said, setting the skillet back on the stovetop.

"And make one for Emma. It's not her usual, but..." I stopped in mid-sentence at Jan's perplexed expression.

"What?" I asked.

Jan wiped her hands on her apron and straightened.

"Honey," she said. "I hate to be the one to tell you this, but Emma left three hours ago."

32

EMMA

I sat in my condo in the armchair in front of the television I never watched.

I typed a text. Deleted it. Typed again. Deleted.

Then I just dropped my phone into my lap and stared into space.

After barely sleeping, I'd gotten up early, put on the clothes I'd worn to work yesterday, and called an Uber.

Fortunately, no one in the Worthington household was awake yet, so I'd just slipped unnoticed out the front door.

Harrison and I were flying to Mackinac Island sometime this morning. A fake honeymoon following a fake wedding.

So I'd dutifully packed a week's worth of clothes. Not knowing what I'd be expected to wear, I'd packed a little bit of everything. Jeans. Casual pants and sweaters. A cocktail dress.

But as I'd packed, my thoughts had raced.

I was getting in too deep. In the span of merely hours, my life had been turned upside down.

Harrison was wanting me to move in with him. I'd never even seen his place.

I had a realistic looking fake tree standing one side of the television. Two magazines I never even opened on the coffee table.

I'd used the marble dining room table, mostly for working, more than anything else, other than the bed, of course. But all my furniture was new and high quality. I'd spent probably twenty thousand dollars on furniture.

And then there was the condo itself. It had taken me two months to get everything done. I'd barely had time to even live here and now he was asking me to live someplace I'd never even seen.

The other alternative was to be deported. Back to Vancouver. Once I was in Canada, I could live anywhere in Canada.

Just not the states.

I didn't want to go back to Canada. I lived here now and had for over ten years.

America was my home.

Canada held nothing but sad memories for me. They say that people forgot the bad things and remembered the good. If that was true, then something was wrong with me.

The pain of loss overshadowed the good memories of my youth.

I couldn't stand the thought of getting close to Harrison, then losing him. Our relationship had an automatic deadline on it. Two years.

We had to pretend to be married for two years. To convince everyone we knew that we were married.

I tapped my phone.

I'd considered telling him that I couldn't go to Mackinac with him. I couldn't go on our fake honeymoon.

But if I didn't go… if I didn't follow through on the fake marriage, then I would go to prison.

I would not do well in prison.

The problem was the more I was around Harrison, the easier it was to pretend.

The pretending was dangerous for me. It was easy to get caught up in it.

And the more I got caught up in it, I knew.

The kisses weren't fake.

33

HARRISON

I pulled up to Emma's condo. Parked in front of her closed garage.

She could be home. Or not.

I stepped out of my car and the early morning breeze brushed my skin. Perfect weather.

Unfortunately, it wouldn't last long before the wrath of the Texas heat would come down on us. And that heat would last far into the months when the rest of the country was experiencing the coolness of fall.

Someone down the street was mowing the grass. The clean fresh scent of freshly mown grass reminded me of my youth when I had my own lawn mowing business. Two days a week mowing neighborhood lawns had given me enough money to cover my video game addiction.

I went up to the front door of Emma's new condo. It was part of a new construction complex.

Modern, clean lines that suited Emma.

Was it wrong to ask her to leave here to go and live with me? Just because my place was bigger? Because I'd been here longer?

Holding my breath, I knocked on the door.

As I'd halfway expected, there was no answer. Her leaving without a word was a sure sign that she didn't want to be bothered.

I knocked again. Louder.

I wasn't going to let her off this easy.

She'd gone through with the wedding, so I was all but certain she didn't want to be deported.

And I was one hundred percent certain she didn't want to go to prison.

I'd gone too far last night. I could admit that. But she was so irresistible.

And she'd been more than willing.

But I was a gentleman and a gentleman was patient.

I'd promised her a marriage of convenience. No strings.

So that was what I was going to give her.

One more time and I was going to leave. Let her come to me.

I held up a hand to knock a third time.

The door opened and Emma stood there looking at me.

"Hi," I said.

"Hi."

"You missed breakfast." I handed her a bag. A familiar bag that she immediately recognized.

Her face brightened.

I'd gone with my gut and brought her an egg and cheese biscuit from the food truck. Her favorite.

"And…" I pulled a coffee from behind my back. "Your latte."

She took the cup and the bag.

"Come in," she said, backing up to give me room to step inside.

I'd been inside before, but I looked at it from a different viewpoint now.

The large designer suitcase and a smaller matching one standing near the door gave me hope.

Her place was uncluttered. New. Even the furniture was new.

Clean.

It was obvious she was a professional woman who was rarely home.

Again, I was plagued by guilt about pulling her away from here.

34

EMMA

*T*he scent of jet fuel filled the air as the small jet, its red Skye Travels logo splashed across the tail, taxied to a stop on the tarmac near us.

The pilot, a woman dressed in a black uniform with a captain's hat opened the door and walked down the stairs.

"Good to see you again, Harrison," she said, shaking his hand, then turning to me. "You must be Emma."

"Emma," Harrison said. "This is Noelle."

"It's a pleasure to meet you, Noelle," I said, shaking her hand.

"Ready to come aboard?" she asked.

"Sure," I said, although I wasn't one hundred percent sure since this was my first time on a private jet.

As we settled into our seats and fastened our belts, I noticed that Harrison seemed comfortable and familiar with the procedure.

"How do you know Noelle?"

"Through Noah," he said, with a shrug.

Right. Of course. He'd worked for Worthington Enterprises

longer than I had and Harrison made friends easily. He knew everybody. That was one of the things that made him such a great assistant. He knew how to get things done. Who to go to and so forth.

I had to remind myself that Harrison was not only my assistant, but he had a degree in architecture and I was supposed to be helping him with some hands-on training.

Since he'd done this for me—kept me from being deported by marrying me—I would make a more concerted effort to share with him what I was doing on my projects and why.

As Noelle took the plane down the runway and we sped up, Harrison reached over and took my hand.

He smiled at me as the plane left the ground and my heart did little flips. It could have been due to the weightlessness of the plane or it could have been Harrison's grin.

Maybe a combination.

Or gazes locked, the sunlight reflecting off his blue eyes, as the plane rose above the trees.

Maybe I was getting in over my head.

Or maybe it was time I took a risk.

I'd willingly married him, knowing that it was a marriage of convenience.

My grandmother's words came back to me as clearly as though she was sitting right next to us.

If you don't take risks, you never really live. Don't be a spectator in life, my dear. Play the game of life with everything you've got.

She'd said that to me when I got my acceptance letter to Harvard.

I'd gone, of course, though there had been times when I regretted it, though what I regretted was never seeing her again.

But I didn't regret actually going and if I had to do it all over again, I would.

Maybe it was time to take my grandmother's advice again. Maybe it also applied to this situation with Harrison.

Play the game. Take a risk.

35

HARRISON

*N*oah and Savannah had been to Mackinac Island on many occasions and Skye Travels even had an airplane there. They were quite familiar.

Savannah had arranged everything. From a horse and carriage to pick us up at the airport to a reservation at the Grand Hotel.

I opened a bottle of champagne and filled two flutes.

"To us," I said, tapping my glass against Emma's.

She smiled a slow smile and took a sip of the champagne.

Maybe it was the altitude, but there was something different in her expression.

Or maybe I was imagining it.

"You've never been?" I asked. "To Mackinac?"

"Never."

"It's a magical place," I said.

"You've been?"

"Once." I didn't elaborate. I didn't tell her that Noah and Savannah had taken me there as a gift when I'd graduated from college.

I wasn't ready to tell her about my relationship with the Worthingtons.

"No cars are allowed," I said. "The only way to get there is by boat or plane."

"Wasn't *Somewhere in Time* filmed there?"

"Yes, it was," I said. "I'm impressed that you know that."

She shrugged and sipped her champagne.

"Anyway, there are no cars on Mackinac."

"None?"

"None."

"How do people get around?"

"They walk, bike, or take a carriage. There's a lot of walking."

"Sounds healthy. Like New York."

"Maybe. I heard they have snow mobiles, but I'm not sure about that. I haven't been in the winter."

"I can't even imagine what winters might be like."

We hit a pocket of turbulence and I instinctively put a hand on Emma's arm.

Holding her glass tightly in her hands, she looked over at me.

"It's okay," I said, released her as the plane leveled out. "Just some turbulence."

"I know," she said. "I'm just not used to small planes."

"You get used to it," I said.

She nodded slowly. "You've flown a lot? Like this? On small jets?"

"Some," I said, dodging the question. "Which city do you like best? Where you've lived?"

She shrugged. "They all have their charm. I like Boston for its old-world charm. New York for its modern hustle and bustle. And Houston… for its friendliness. How about you?"

"I like Houston," I said. "I have family in Los Angeles, but other than to see them, I'd never go there."

She looked blankly at me a moment.

"Did you tell your family you got married?"

"Not yet," I said.

She turned away, looking out the window.

I was having a hard time understanding this beautiful woman I'd married.

One thing, however, I did understand.

As we interacted away from the office, she was learning more and more things about me. Things that I rarely thought about. Like traveling in private jets. Truth was, I'd never flown commercial.

I wasn't going to be able to keep my true identity from her for very much longer.

36

EMMA

*B*efore we landed at the Mackinac airport, Noelle made a scenic swoop around the island.

The Grand Hotel, sporting the longest porch in the world, was stunningly beautiful. Lovely lilac flowers were everywhere.

After a perfect landing, we taxied to the little terminal and Noelle opened the plane's door.

Harrison went down the steps first, then took my hand and helped me down.

The weather was chilly, but the sun was warm. And somehow the scent of flowers overshadowed the scent of jet fuel.

A horse and buggy with a formally dressed driver waited for us.

"What about our luggage?" I asked.

"It'll be at the hotel when we get there. We get to take the scenic route."

After I got on board the buggy, Harrison tucked a blanket over my legs, then asked me to wait.

"I need to talk to Noelle for just a minute," he said.

I couldn't hear what they were talking about, so I checked

to see if I had any messages. I did not. It seemed like the world knew that I was on my honeymoon and left me alone.

"First time to Mackinac?" the driver asked, pulling me away from my phone.

"Yes," I said. "It's beautiful."

"One of the most beautiful places in the world," he said. "It's gonna be cold tonight, though. Hope you brought something warm to wear."

"Just a sweater," I said.

"You'll be alright. The hotel is always warm."

Harrison was jogging back toward the buggy and Noelle went inside the terminal.

"They tell me this is your honeymoon," the driver said as Harrison climbed into the buggy.

"That's right," Harrison said, wrapping an arm around me. "Married last night."

"Congratulations," the driver said. "You picked a wonderful spot for your honeymoon."

I leaned against Harrison and he took part of the blanket.

Snuggled together, we rode past little cottages. I couldn't imagine people actually living here, but they did. There were clothes hanging on clotheslines and tricycles in the backyard.

It felt so right being here with Harrison.

There were so many things I was learning about him that didn't fit what I thought I knew. Like how he was accustomed to flying on private jets. How he'd been to Mackinac Island before. How he knew Noah and Savannah well enough that they pulled off a last minute wedding for us... even knowing that it was a marriage of convenience to keep me here.

"Emma," Harrison said.

"Yes?"

"Can you do something for me? Just for the rest of the day?"

"I'll try. What is it?"

He pressed a finger against my brow and gently massaged

it. My eyes closed and I knew that whatever it was he was asking I would be powerless not to do it.

"Will you stop worrying? Just for the rest of the day? Tonight?"

I nodded and took a deep breath.

I could do that. Surely I could do that.

Just one night.

37

HARRISON

I paced back and forth in the parlor while I waited for Emma to come out of her bedroom.

Each room in the Grand Hotel had a different theme. This particular theme was pink and green—an odd combination that actually went surprisingly well together and was pleasing to the eye.

I was wearing a suit and tie now. The clerk at the front desk had made sure that we knew dinner required formal attire.

It was too early for dinner, but Emma and I had come to our suite to rest. Tomorrow we would venture into town. We had a week here. I'd spent most of the last hour rescheduling Emma's calls and meetings.

She hadn't seemed too happy with taking a week off work, but I'd convinced her that it was expected of a newly married couple.

Then I'd reminded her that she could worry about it tomorrow. That the rest of the day she wasn't to worry.

I was secretly hoping that once she got the of hang of not worrying, she would continue to do so. That she would relax and we could enjoy our time here.

The more time I spent with her, the more I liked her and the more I wanted to be with her. Even now, with her in the next room, I paced, ready to see her again.

If it was possible, it seemed like there had been an attraction simmering just below the surface and with just a little bit of encouragement, that attraction had become full blown.

The windows were open, the soft breeze bringing the scent of lilacs with it.

The mournful horn of a ferry taking day visitors back to the mainland, drifted across the water.

I had appreciated the beauty of the island the first time I'd visited, but now, being here with Emma, I saw it completely differently. Now I appreciated the romanticism of it.

There was an air of magic surrounding it. Maybe it came from the history of it. Maybe it came from the movie *Somewhere in Time* that had been filmed here years ago. Or maybe it was just being here with Emma.

Whatever it was, I wanted to see and do everything with Emma.

Her bedroom door opened and she stepped out. She was wearing a sleek solid black dress with a sweetheart neckline. Her hair was down, just like it had been yesterday.

And again, I was struck with not only how beautiful she was, but how I hadn't noticed it before this week.

How had she been right in front of me and I hadn't even realized just how beautiful she was?

"You're beautiful," I said, stepping toward her.

She smiled, biting her lip, and looked at me with those stunningly clear green eyes. Eyes that I wanted to fall into.

"You're kinda pretty yourself."

I laughed. "Nobody's accused me of that before."

"Well, maybe you've been hanging out with the wrong person."

I took her hand and led her out the door before I did something crazy like kiss her again.

38

EMMA

I watched Harrison out of the corner of my eye as the elevator gently swayed its way to the ground floor.

When I'd said he was pretty, I'd done him an injustice. He was as handsome as any man I'd ever met and that was saying a lot considering I worked in a male dominated world—both architects and construction workers. He was dressed in a suit and tie, much like he wore to work, yet something seemed different about him. Maybe it was because we weren't at the office. It was normal for people to look different in a different setting.

Or maybe it was because we were in a beautiful historical hotel on a beautiful one of a kind island.

Or maybe it was because it was starting to sink in that I was married to him.

Somehow, by a seemingly accidental turn of events, I'd ended up married to one of the most handsome men I could ever imagine.

Had I been attracted to him all along?

If I had been, I hadn't realized it or... maybe I hadn't acknowledged it.

Either way, I was most definitely attracted to him now.

He was still lightly holding my hand in his. Casual. Like we'd been together for ages and were comfortably in love.

The elevator doors opened and, stepping out, we walked down the hallway toward the restaurant.

Live music grew louder as we walked along the wide hallway.

Letting Harrison lead the way, we reached the lobby and detoured out the doors onto the famous porch.

"It's going to be a beautiful sunset," he said, going to stand at the rail that overlooked the gardens and the lake in the distance. The lake looked more like an ocean from here.

As I put my left hand on the rail, sunlight glinted off my diamond ring—a perfect diamond.

Turning my face up to the sunset, I could let myself believe in the fairytale for just one night. I couldn't think of a logical reason why I couldn't.

For just one night I could truly be Mrs. Harrison Moore.

For just one night I could pretend that the marriage was real.

What harm could it do?

"I'll go get us something to drink," he said, kissing the back of my hand before letting go and walking back toward the doors.

I sat down on a bench and leaned forward.

Instead of looking out at the view, however, I studied the diamond ring on my finger.

The marriage had been real. We'd had a real priest. A real marriage license.

It followed that the honeymoon would be real. Sort of.

I shook my head and leaned back.

Letting my thoughts go down this path would get me into trouble.

It was okay to have a crush on my fake husband.

It was not okay to sleep with him.

And it certainly wasn't okay to fall in love with him.

And I knew myself well enough to know that one would follow the other.

And it didn't matter which one came first.

Harrison returned with two glasses of champagne.

"They insisted we have champagne," he said. "for our honeymoon."

"How did they know?" I asked, taking one of the flutes from him.

"I don't know," he shrugged. "It's a small island." He sat down next to me. "And I've heard it's a magical place."

Maybe that was it.

Maybe Mackinac Island was a magical place.

39

HARRISON

The island seemed quieter without the day tourists walking about just being tourists. Maybe it was actually quieter simply because there were fewer people on the island and it followed that there were fewer people in the hotel.

I didn't tell Emma that Noah and Savannah were regular guests here. That the Worthingtons had called again to make sure we had champagne.

I was going to have to tell her eventually that they were my godparents.

The longer I avoided it, the worse it was going to be.

It had started off as a simple avoidance. But now it was starting to feel like I was lying to her.

I wanted to tell her everything.

And being Noah's godson was a big part of my identity.

But for now, at least, I would take my own advice.

I would not worry about it tonight.

I could take the day off from worrying.

In fact, I decided, I could wait until we got back to Houston to worry about it.

There was no point in wasting a perfectly good honeymoon

on Mackinac Island with worrying about things like revealing my true identity to the woman I'd married.

Maybe I could focus on getting to know her instead of worrying about telling her who I was.

Feeling like a teenager getting time alone with his girlfriend, I slid an arm around her shoulders and we sat silently watching as the last ferryboat of the day, packed with the day tourists, heading out across the lake.

"I wonder what it would be like to live here," she said.

"I've always wondered that, too. It seems like it would be relaxing, doesn't it?"

"I'm sure they have their own stresses."

I smiled over at her. "I'm sure they do, but I like to think of it as being a stress-free place."

She laughed. "Does that even exist?"

I took a sip of champagne. Considered.

"I think that moments like that exist. And if we can string enough of those moments together, then life feels less stressful."

She leaned her head against my shoulder.

Moments like this.

"I think you're right," she said. "I'm all for having a string of stress-free moments."

I kissed her on the side of her forehead.

And I wondered. I wondered if being married to Emma was the start of a string of stress-free moments. Or maybe even something more.

Whatever it was, I was happy to see that she was relaxing around me and seemed to be starting to trust me.

I liked this side of her.

I had been so close to not taking advantage of helping her. To continuing to believe that she was cold and distant.

Taking her left hand in mine, I ran a finger over the simple diamond ring that said it all.

40

EMMA

*O*ur hotel suite at the Grand Hotel had one main room and two bedrooms. The bedroom Harrison was decorated in a pretty pale green, the color of a granny smith apple. My bedroom was decorated in pink and the main room was done in a mixture of the two colors.

I liked the way the designer had pulled it all together and I could only imagine the work that had gone into decorating each room, especially since each room had a different color scheme or theme. Three hundred ninety-seven unique rooms.

Each room had a different name, many named after former first ladies.

I'd done some quick research on the hotel to refresh my memory from college. It opened its door in 1887 after taking just over three months to complete. A remarkable feat. Since that time, a couple of wings had been added.

The pictures and floorplans we'd studied didn't do it justice.

I'd changed into my pajama bottoms and tee-shirt, then added a sweatshirt.

Not exactly typical honeymoon fashion.

I sat at the vanity and ran a brush through my hair.

It wasn't exactly a typical honeymoon either.

I got all tingly inside when I thought about kissing Harrison.

Putting the brush down, I took a deep breath and looked myself in the eye.

I liked Harrison. Liked as in liked. *That way.*

Before all this deportation stuff had started happening, I hadn't thought about him *that* way. I would have been blind to not have noticed that he was handsome, but I had a particularly stalwart shield when it came to men.

Three of my fellow female classmates had gotten married and given up their careers before they'd even gotten off the ground.

This was different.

I had my career.

I wasn't giving up anything by marrying Harrison.

Instead I was gaining everything.

Not only was I allowed to stay in America, I was married to the guy I was crushing on.

Just one night.

I would allow myself to pretend for just one night that this was a real marriage.

It would be a waste of a perfectly good honeymoon not to at least stay up and have a glass of champagne with my husband.

Tomorrow... or maybe the next day... there would be time to sort everything out.

Feeling a bit chilly, I closed my window.

I plugged in my cell phone on the nightstand and left it to charge while I went out into the main room to have a drink with my new husband.

Shields up.

Yes, he was handsome.
Yes, he was my husband.
Yes, I wanted to kiss him again.
But I would not fall in love with him.
Not even an option.

41

HARRISON

I paced from one side of the room to the other and back again.

I stopped at the window and pressed my hands against the ledge. The full moon hung low over the lake, casting a brilliant glow on the water.

If I could paint, I would want to capture this moment on canvas. I could take a picture, sure, but a photograph was less intimate and wouldn't do the image justice.

A painting could capture the essence of the moment.

A moment in time.

I needed—wanted—to convince Emma that we could be more than fake husband and wife, but I knew that the idea had to grow from the seeds that had been planted.

Her door opened and she stepped out. She was wearing gray pajama bottoms and a dark gray Harvard sweatshirt.

She was absolutely adorable, but she stood there looking at me with uncertainty.

I walked to her and wrapped my arms around her.

She wrapped her arms around my waist and laid her cheek against my chest.

I closed my eyes and savored the moment.

I'd asked her to give me just one night of no worry. She was giving me that.

And as hard as it was not to take advantage of that, I would not.

It was a struggle for me because my intentions were pure and I have every intention of keeping her if she'd have me.

I scooped her up and carried her to the sofa. I sat, keeping her nestled in my lap.

I kissed the top of her head and held her close.

"It's cold outside," she said.

"You don't have to go." I held her closer.

She laughed softly as I'd hoped she would.

"I'll stay," she said.

"Do you want a drink?" I asked.

"No, I'm good."

"Hot chocolate?"

"Maybe later."

I looked over her head at the moon.

"How about the moon?"

"The what?" She lifted her head and looked at me.

"The moon," I said. "I could lasso it down here and give it to you."

"Alright, James Stewart. You go right ahead and do that." She was smiling at me.

I kissed her forehead.

"Surely there's something I can get you."

"There is something," she said, looking into my eyes.

"Anything."

"Kiss me."

I didn't even have to think about it.

It was as though I'd been waiting my whole life for that simple request.

42

EMMA

The moonlight streamed in through the window, casting a soft sparkly glow across the room.

The open window brought not only a soft breeze, but also the scent of fresh flowers.

It was quiet. No distant roar of automobiles or trains or planes. Just quiet. If I listened really close, I could almost hear the water lapping along the beach. I could definitely hear a fog horn in the distance.

I was drunk on Harrison's kisses. He held me in his lap, one hand keeping me firmly in place, the other splayed across my cheek, touching my lips, sending my nerves endings into a fever.

My fingers tugged lightly at his hair and I arched toward him, trying to get closer.

He had my senses coiled and centered at my core.

"What have you done to me?" he asked between kisses.

"Me?" I couldn't catch my breath enough to say anything more.

He trailed kisses across my cheek to run his tongue around

the inner curves of my ear, sending shards of pleasure through me.

I moaned. This was too much.

My lips ached with missing him. I turned my head and captured his lips again.

His tongue touched the roof of my mouth and I shivered.

I'm not sure if he did it or if I did it, but I shifted so that I was straddling him.

With something that sounded like a growl, he pulled me closer.

I felt him beneath me... wanting me...

Our lips and tongues tangling together, I moved against him until everything else faded away and I gave in to the pleasure of being with him.

I moved, letting myself go.

A moment later, I exploded against him with a little whimper.

He held me close as I came back to earth, placing little kisses across my face.

I went limp against him, my cheek against his shoulder. He smelled like musky vanilla... spruce... whatever it was, it was completely male.

He held me that way as the moon rose high into the sky, leaving us in darkness.

In a smooth motion, he lay back on the sofa, bringing me with him.

He held me tightly against him and I'd never felt so safe as I felt right now.

I drifted to sleep in his arms to the sound of a distant foghorn and waves lapping against the lake's beach that I may or may not have imagined.

I was pretty sure I had died and gone to heaven.

Right before my very eyes, my fake marriage had morphed into a something real.

A real kiss.

And I'd done exactly what I'd promised myself I wouldn't do.

I'd gone and fell in love with my fake husband.

The marriage might be fake.

But the falling in love part was real.

43

HARRISON

*S*ometimes being a gentleman was sorely overrated.

After my hands finishing up what I'd started with Emma, I stepped out of the steamy shower and dried off.

I cared more about her than satisfying my own lust.

That would come later, when she was ready.

She'd come to me willingly, giving me exactly what I'd asked for. One worry-free night.

I had plans for today. She never took time off except to work out. Time off to work out.

What I had in mind for today would satisfy her need for exercise as well as give us some time alone in nature.

I wasn't going to pressure her.

I was going to stay true to my intensions. A marriage with no strings.

When I'd asked for time to work on my own projects, I'd known that would come anyway. It had simply been a place filler. To give us both a logical reason for what I was offering.

In retrospect, I had gone with my gut and following the unacknowledged attraction I'd held for her all along.

It was funny how it had turned on a dime. Love was like that, though. Sometimes it grew softly and sometimes it came like a sucker punch.

This thing with Emma was a double whammy. It had started off slowly, then punched me in the gut.

That had to be the most powerful kind of love. I was caught in her web. Happily.

Now all I had to do was to convince her that I was worthy of being her husband. Not just in name, but in reality.

I didn't want that two-year deadline. I wanted a forever deadline.

We could have babies and grow old together. Like Noah and Savannah... without being separated for a ton of years.

I pulled on my jeans and a sweatshirt. Then put on a hoody.

The mornings on Mackinac were chilly, but when the sun came out, it would heat things up.

Ready to go, I opened the door and stepped out into the main room.

Emma had still been asleep on the sofa when I'd gone into my bedroom to shower.

The blanket I'd left her with was folded and left on the chair.

I heard the hair dryer going in the other room.

Smiling to myself, I sat on the sofa and turned on the television.

Flipping channels, I found a baseball game. I didn't consider myself an avid sports fan, but I liked a good game as well as the next guy.

I settled back on the sofa to wait.

We weren't at home, but the suite felt close enough that I could imagine what a typical day with Emma would be like.

Like today, we'd get ready for work. We could even work together like we did now, except we would both be architects. I could imagine that we'd have some engaging conversations about architecture.

My mind wandered down that fantasy for a while as Emma got ready and the baseball game played on the television.

If everything could stay just like this, I would be content.

44

EMMA

I straightened my hair, adding little flips at the ends and left it down around my shoulders.

It was too much. So I grabbed a scrunchie and pulled it back into a long ponytail.

I added some mascara to my lashes.

It was like I was getting ready to go on a date.

And I sort of was.

A date with my husband.

I started to add some blush, then decided my face was flushed enough without it.

I had no idea what he had planned for today, but I wasn't particularly worried about it. Whatever it was, it would be with Harrison and that made me happy.

I decided to wear a loose light green cotton skirt with a white tee-shirt tucked in. Then I added a chambray shirt, tying it at the waist.

A straw hat would have perfected the look, but I didn't have one. I actually didn't have a lot of casual clothes. This was probably the best casual outfit I had.

Deciding I was good to go, I took a deep breath, grabbed my phone, and headed out to the main room.

Going with a quick impulse, I pulled the scrunchie out of my hair, letting my hair fall where it may around my shoulders.

Harrison was sitting on the sofa, feet propped up, watching a baseball game.

I had a flash of how my life could look.

Normal.

Normal was not something I had ever had. At least not as an adult. As a child yes, but it was such a distant memory, I'd begun to doubt that normal would ever be a reality for me.

He looked and smiled.

My heart fluttered like a thousand butterflies had been let loose in my chest.

This man set my senses on fire.

Although I returned his smile, I held my hands together to keep them from trembling.

"Did you sleep well enough?" he asked. "considering that you were on the sofa."

"Well enough." I had slept surprisingly well, but I didn't want to tell him that. I didn't want to tell him that I had slept like a baby in his arms, feeling content and safe.

He stood up and walked straight to me, pulling me into a hug.

All my resolve to be cool dissolved just like that.

"You look beautiful," he said, tilting my chin up and placing a chaste kiss on my lips.

"Thank you."

"Are you hungry?"

"A little." Why was Harrison always trying to feed me? Traditional gender roles suggested that I should be the one feeding him.

"Good," he said. "Because the hotel has the best mimosas in the country."

"I'm not surprised." I smiled as he took my hand and led me toward the door. "What are we doing today?"

"I have a grand surprise for you," he said with a little wink that melted my heart.

Whatever it was, I was sure it would be enjoyable. As long as it was with him.

I was most definitely in over my head on this one.

I knew this feeling well enough.

I was falling in love with Harrison.

45

HARRISON

*T*he only sounds came from the gentle lapping of the water against the shoreline and the steady rumble of the bicycle tires against the dirt road and the clicking of the spokes. The distant wail of a ferry echoed from the distance.

I had turkey sandwiches, potato salad, and a fruit bowl in a basket behind me. Emma had extra bottles of water in her basket.

She looked adorable wearing her full light green skirt and blue shirt tied at the waist.

After we had breakfast at the hotel, they had packed us a lunch for our bicycle trip around the island.

We were about halfway around the island when I spotted what looked like a perfectly secluded spot for a leisurely picnic.

We stopped and leaned our bicycles against a tree. The wind breezed through the newly budded leaves of the trees.

Emma, standing at the edge of the lake, glancing at me over her shoulder.

I spread a red and white checkered cloth on the ground and set both baskets on it.

Then I put my hands on my hips and watched Emma.

She took off her canvas sneakers and, holding them by the shoestrings, stuck her toes in the water.

"It's cold," she said, looking back at me.

"Of course, it is," I said on a chuckle.

She rolled her eyes at me and turned back, pulling her hair to one side.

Unable to keep my hands off her, I went up behind her and swept her off her feet.

She laughed as I twirled her around. After setting her on her feet, I kissed her neck, breathing in her clean jasmine scent.

I took a step forward and went to set her back down in the water.

"Wait," she said, laughing and pulling her feet up.

"No?"

"No. It's cold."

"Okay," I said, twirling her the other way and setting her on her feet.

"You're terrible," she said.

"Yeah?" I put a finger beneath her chin and tilted her face up to mine.

The bright sunlight sparkled in her lovely green eyes. I tangled my fingers in her hair and put a hand behind her neck.

"Am I terrible at this?" I kissed her lightly on her lips.

"No," she whispered, her eyes drifting closed.

"No?"

She leaned forward and I wrapped my arms around her to pull her against me.

I pressed my lips against hers, letting the sensations flow through me.

I couldn't get enough of this girl.

I deepened the kiss, my tongue sliding over hers.

She was my wife.

And I was going to court her until she agreed to be mine.

46

EMMA

*T*he sunlight was warm on my back and the breeze cool. Sensations I remembered from growing up in Vancouver.

But unlike Vancouver, it was so peaceful. So quiet.

Just the lap of the water against the shore. The distant sound of a ferry boat horn.

Wispy clouds drifted lazily by creating barely noticeable shadows.

I lay on the picnic blanket with my head cushioned on Harrison's thigh. He leaned against a tree, fingers toying with my hair.

I never wanted to move.

"Where do you see yourself in five years?" Harrison asked.

"What?" I turned my head to glance back at him. "Is this an interview?"

He laughed. "Maybe. Since we're married, I need to know these things about you." He shrugged. "Just in case anyone asks."

That actually made sense.

"I've never told anybody."

"Why not?

"It's… ambitious."

And risky.

"I have some ambitions."

There were so many things I didn't know about Harrison. As I spent more time with him he was becoming so much more than just my assistant.

"I'm thinking about starting my own company," I blurted.

"As an architect?"

"Is there anything else?" I laughed.

"Not in my world."

"Mine either."

The sun was starting its descent over the horizon. As much as I hated it, I knew we had to get up and leave soon. Riding a bicycle in the dark didn't suit my cautious nature.

"I wouldn't mind doing that, too," Harrison said.

I looked up at him again. "Starting your own business?"

"Sure. Why not?"

I nodded.

"Is that one of your ambitions?"

"It is." He ran a finger down my cheek. "One of many."

"What are some of your other ambitions?"

"Oh, I don't know. A house or a condo. A family."

I forced myself to breath.

I imagined a couple of children running around, laughing, while Harrison and I sat just like this. I wasn't opposed to children. I was just waiting for the right time.

"Do you have a timeline for that?" I asked.

"A timeline? No. That's something that just happens. I think putting love and kids on a timeline would suck all the joy out."

"I guess it could."

"Do you have a timeline?"

"No. And if I did, it would be off the tracks now."

He didn't say anything.

Had I taken two years away from his personal life?

If he planned on having kids, was I standing in his way?

47

HARRISON

*W*e sat at a white-clothed table for dinner. She was wearing her solid black dress, her hair pulled over her left shoulder and clipped.

Her eyes were bright and her lips were shiny and plump. Begging to be kissed.

My stomach grumbled at the scent of fresh baked bread.

"Champagne?" I asked as the server headed our way.

"I'd like a martini," Emma said.

"Oh. A martini," I said with a little wink. "Feeling adventurous?"

"Maybe," she said. "All that fresh air."

Our gazes held until the server stopped at our table.

"Mr. Moore?" the young lady said.

"Yes." The girl looked vaguely familiar, though to save my life, I couldn't place where I'd seen her.

"We met when you were here with Mr. and Mrs. Worthington." She smiled. "You might remember my mother. She owns the new bridal shop in town."

"Right," I said. I did remember meeting the woman who owned the shop in town. She'd made an impression because she'd started such a unique shop on the island. I didn't, however, remember meeting her daughter, but not surprising since the girl was a teenager.

"How are you?" I asked.

"Great," she said. "I'm going to college in the fall."

"Wonderful," I said. I couldn't remember the girl's name. "This is my wife, Emma."

"Nice to meet you," the girl said. "Drinks?"

I ordered our drinks and the girl left.

"I'm sorry," I said to Emma. "I can't remember her name."

"It's okay," Emma said, with a tight smile, her gaze flicking away from mine.

"She's just a teenager."

"I know," she said, glancing back at me. "You came here with Noah and Savannah?"

I guess today was as good a day as any to tell her about my relationship with Noah and Savannah.

"I did. They brought me here when I graduated from college."

She looked decidedly alarmed.

"I don't understand. Why would they do that?"

She was looking directly at me now, her eyes wide, waiting for an answer.

"I need to tell you something," I said, leaning forward. "I was going to wait until we got home, but it looks like we're going to be talking about it now."

The girl brought our drinks, both martinis.

I took a sip. Braced myself.

Emma held her drink in both hands, slowly twirling the stem.

"Noah and Savannah are my godparents."

"Godparents? They must know your parents."

"Yeah," I said with a little laugh. "My mother is Noah's ex-wife."

"Oh." She looked at me sideways and sipped her drink. "Well, that explains a lot."

"I guess it does."

"This is a really good martini." She ate an olive off the toothpick.

I'd expected some kind of reaction. Certainly more than *that explains a lot.*

And to think that I had fretted over how to tell her this whole time.

That was the thing about fretting. It was rarely necessary.

48

EMMA

The martini was cold and salty. It was perfection. Since I didn't like to have my thinking muddled, I rarely drank alcohol.

But tonight was one of those occasions when it seemed like the thing to do.

The restaurant was about half full, everyone dressed formally. Conversation blended with faint music in the background.

It was similar to what I imagined a cruise would be like, although I'd never been on a cruise.

"Want another drink?" Harrison asked.

I looked down at my empty glass. Shook my head.

If I had another drink, I would drink it. But I was already feeling the effects of this one.

"So," I said. "If you're Noah's godchild, why are you working as my assistant?"

"Good question." His glass was still half full.

"Noah believes in starting at the bottom of the company and working up."

"I see." So the plan was for Harrison to work his way up in the company. And he was starting out as my assistant.

For some reason, that made me feel used. Like I was just a stepping stone.

"So you're going to be working your way up in the company."

"It wasn't my idea." He leaned back in his chair.

Nonetheless, he was going to go right on past me. Not that I cared about that. I had no aspirations to be in management.

But I had entertained some fantasies about working with Harrison. Side by side just as we had been since I'd started this job in Houston.

I would have to think about it later.

"My lips are numb," I said.

He smiled that slow smile that charmed me every time.

"Is that so?"

"Yes." I licked my lips.

"Are you sure?"

"Positive," I said.

"Let me see." He leaned forward. Put a hand beneath my chin.

My eyes drifted closed and he pressed his lips against mine.

"You don't feel that, then?" he whispered against my lips.

"Yes, I…"

His lips fused to mine before I knew what he intended.

He kissed me right there in front of everyone and I more than felt it.

I was swept away.

I hadn't meant to be. I had meant to maintain my distance.

My fingertip dug into his shoulders and the rest of the world faded away.

He was related, in an odd way, to the Worthingtons. I would have to think about that and about what it meant. But I would have to think about it later.

Right now I couldn't think about anything except the way his lips felt against mine.

And that I couldn't get enough of this man.

My husband.

49

HARRISON

*a*s we neared our hotel door, I picked Emma up to carry her across the threshold.

It was not an easy accomplishment considering that I had to dig the old-fashioned key out of my pocket to unlock the door.

Emma giggled as I let her slide to her feet for half a moment, but she kept her arms around my neck and I picked her up again and kicked the door closed.

Light green curtains fluttered at the window we'd left open. Now that the sun had gone done, it was cold.

I again let her slide to her feet when we reached the sofa. Then I pulled her into my lap and wrapped a wool throw around us both.

Wrapping my arms around her, I pulled her close against me and pressed my lips against hers. Then I dipped my tongue inside her mouth for a better taste of her.

I could not get enough.

She'd only had one martini, but she'd laughed like a schoolgirl all the way upstairs. I was enchanted by her laughter. Something I'd never heard before today.

"Emma," I breathed against her ear before I kissed her earlobe.

"Hmm?"

"I have to tell you something."

"Okay," she said, turning her head to capture my lips.

I forgot what I was going to say.

She tasted so good.

I never wanted to stop kissing her.

She was pushing for more. I could feel it in the way she ran the tips of her fingers across my back. The way she leaned her head back, as I trailed kisses down her neck.

But I was a gentleman and I was going to treat her as a lady.

I liked her too much to want her to have regrets in the morning.

We may be married, but we hadn't exactly married for this.

I had, in fact, promised her a no strings attached marriage of convenience.

I would never forgive myself for pushing something on her she wasn't ready for. Especially not when she was tipsy like this.

Shifting, I laid her back on the couch. Though she looked at me through hooded eyes, I merely tucked her feet in my lap and pulled off her shoes.

Then I began massaging her feet. I started lightly rubbing her toes, moving my way up to her foot. Then I started with her other foot.

She relaxed and closed her eyes.

I massaged her feet until she fell asleep.

I tucked the blanket around her and knelt on the floor next to her.

Sweeping a strand of hair off her forehead, I kissed her gently on the lips.

She stirred a little, but didn't wake up.

"So what I was going to tell you was…" I took a deep breath. "I'm so falling in love with you."

A little smile may have crossed her features.

Or maybe I imagined it.

50

EMMA

$\mathcal{I}$ woke disoriented and quickly realized I was on a sofa. It was quiet. Perfectly quiet.

And I was not only lying on a sofa, but I was under an unfamiliar blanket.

The window was closed, but the air was cold.

Piece by piece, the events of last night started coming back to me.

Harrison.

And kissing.

Lots of kissing.

I pressed my fingers over my swollen lips.

There had definitely been kissing… and lots of it.

And he had told me something.

I sat up and went in search of water.

I found a bottle of water sitting on the mini-bar and drank it down.

Harrison had told me that he was Noah and Savannah's godson.

I walked back and dropped onto the sofa. What was it he'd said? His mother was Noah's ex-wife.

I should have known something was off after the way he'd pulled together that wedding... at Noah's house.

What had I done?

I'd married the boss's... stepson? What was the correct terminology. He'd called himself a godson.

So that's what he was.

Good heavens.

That meant that Harrison was automatically headed up the corporate ladder.

And I was merely a stepping stone.

But now that he'd married me, what did that mean?

I'd been thinking that we could work together, but now working together didn't seem so likely. Not when he was related—sort of—to the big boss.

When I jumped into the water, I dove straight down.

What was I supposed to do now?

How was I supposed to act around him?

Especially since there had been so much kissing.

Had there been more?

No. Definitely not. I would remember that.

I ran a hand through my hair. I needed a shower.

I would remember if there had been more.

After turning on the hot water, I gathered up my clothes. Today I would wear my other casual outfit. A breezy white skirt and a light blue sweater set.

My thoughts were full of Harrison.

Working with him.

Laughing with him.

Kissing him.

Our relationship had changed so quickly. But that was how it happened, right?

I wasn't even sure we'd liked each other before he'd stepped in to keep me from being deported.

I'd liked him, but I wasn't sure he'd liked me. I was his boss and he was my assistant. I hadn't exactly been all that friendly towards him.

It had been a defense, I admitted to myself. A defense to keep me from being attracted to him.

It obviously hadn't worked.

I was charmed by him. Charmed and spellbound.

I stepped into the shower, and just stood beneath the spray of hot water. Letting it waken my senses and get my thoughts going.

Harrison had married me out of kindness.

I mustn't forget that.

And reminding myself of that shattered my heart.

And that's how I knew. I was falling in love with him.

51

HARRISON

I walked along the shoreline of the Lake Huron. The clear blue water sparkled in the morning sunlight.

Stopping to sit on one of the wooden benches, I sipped my vanilla latte. I had always been a cold coffee kind of guy, but Emma had inadvertently converted me to lattes.

Besides, the warm coffee was a nice way to warm up from the inside to combat the chilly morning air.

I'd left Emma sleeping on the sofa. I'd thought about carrying her to her own bed, but she'd looked so comfortable I didn't want to risk waking her.

I pulled out my phone and facetimed my mother.

"Hi, Harrison." Claire Moore looked good. As always. She claimed that she'd been happy since the day she'd reconnected with my father.

Her marriage to Noah Worthington had been arranged by their parents. I never really understood why someone would consent to such an arrangement.

And then I'd turned around and done the same thing myself.

I'd married out of convenience.

I just hoped that mine turned out better than hers.

"Hi Momma. How are you?"

"I'm good, honey." She squinted at the phone. "Where are you?"

"Mackinac Island."

"Oh. Are you there for work?"

"Sort of," I said.

"What's bothering you?"

Momma knew her children. I had to give her that.

I took a deep breath.

"I've gotten myself into a... situation."

"I see," she said, sitting down at her breakfast table. Still wearing her robe, she hadn't been up long. It was barely six o'clock in Los Angeles. "Want to tell me about it?"

"Not really," I said. "But I need your help."

"I'll do what I can."

The first ferry boat of the day, packed with tourists, approached the dock, mournful whistle blowing. The morning mist was barely visible over the lake now.

I would need to get back soon... before Emma woke to find me gone.

I'd stop by and get coffee for her. Maybe some breakfast.

"Harrison?"

"Sorry," I said. "Momma. I got married."

Momma's mouth dropped open. I had to give Noah credit for not telling her.

"I didn't know you were seeing anyone," she said. "Not since..."

"I wasn't."

"Then...?"

I could see her mind working out possibilities.

I knew that she was thinking about my older half-sister, Daniella, who had gotten accidentally gotten pregnant by someone else before she met her husband.

"It's not that," I said. "She needed my help. I'll tell you everything. But I really need your help with something else."

"I'm listening."

"I married her to help her... but now I actually want to be married to her."

I took a deep breath and looked toward the horizon.

"I've fallen in love with her."

52

EMMA

I took my time getting dressed. Put on some light makeup and straightened my hair.

I knocked on Harrison's door, but he didn't answer.

Pressing my hands against my waist, I fought the panic that shot through me.

He wouldn't have left me here. It wasn't his nature.

Even if he did, I could find my way home.

Turning the knob, I slowly pushed the door open.

Seeing his things still there, relief flooded through me. But Harrison wasn't there.

I shouldn't be here. Harrison was surprisingly unorganized. He must use up all his organizational energy at work.

His suitcase was open, clothes scattered there and across the back of the chair. It looked like he must have kicked his shoes aside and just left them there.

I started to turn. To go back into the main room and wait. Maybe I'd even go downstairs for coffee.

But something in his suitcase caught my attention.

I couldn't help myself.

I slowly walked to the suitcase and picked up the photograph.

It was a picture of Harrison and a very pretty young lady standing in front of the Christmas tree in the Houston Galleria.

I'd stood in almost his same spot in early January short after I first arrived in Houston.

The girl was smiling as Harrison kissed her on the cheek.

If it had been anyone other than Harrison, I would called it a charming photograph.

Instead, it stabbed me in the heart.

They were so obviously happy and in love.

I turned the photograph over. It was signed.

Love you forever, Christy.

I dropped the photograph as though it had burned me.

I whirled around and blindly darted from his room.

I never should have gone into his room, much less picked up a photo from his suitcase.

But I had. And now I knew.

The thing I had worried about was true.

I'd taken Harrison away from someone he loved.

He'd married me out of either a sense of duty or pity, all the while being in love with someone else.

Someone named Christy.

I grabbed my purse, looped it over my shoulder, and headed out of the room.

Running blindly, I took the stairs instead of the elevator.

I dashed outside onto the porch, down the steps, to the garden area.

Slowing, I caught my breath.

Beautiful flowers bloomed along the path. It was so pretty here. So romantic.

I stopped and ran my fingers along the petals of a white rose. Breathed in its sweet scent.

That's when I realized tears were falling down my cheeks.

I swiped them away.

I would not cry.

I'd known better than to let myself feel something for Harrison.

I was smarter than that.

I'd known what I was doing when I did it.

I'd married Harrison to keep from being deported.

Nothing more. Nothing less.

We'd get the marriage annulled.

It was the right thing to do.

I had to let Harrison off the hook so he could be with Christy.

I would fix it and I would go back to Vancouver.

I had to do what was right.

53

HARRISON

I whistled to myself as I walked down the long hallway to our room.

My mother was good at seeing things clearly when all I could see was disaster.

My good mood vanished, though, when I got to the room and found that Emma wasn't there. Her door was open and her purse was gone.

I didn't blame her for not waiting for me.

I'd been gone a lot longer than I'd planned.

I set her coffee and biscuit on the table and pulled out my phone.

ME: *Good morning.*

ME: *I went to get us coffee and time got away.*

I waited, but got no response.

ME: *Where are you?*

No answer.

She probably went downstairs to get her own coffee and breakfast.

Leaving the biscuit, but taking the coffee with me, I locked up and headed out.

The hotel was big, but it wasn't so big that I couldn't find Emma.

Besides, I had turned on her phone locator.

I'd never used it, but it was there if I needed it and in a case like this, I would do what needed to be done.

She wasn't in the restaurant and she wasn't in the lobby or out on the porch.

The coffee was cold, so I tossed in the nearest wastebasket.

I would get her another if she wanted.

I even stopped at the front desk, but the clerk hadn't seen her.

He suggested I try the gardens.

Emma could have gone for a run. She did that sometimes.

I needed to slow down and not panic. She was a grown woman. And she was here somewhere. Her luggage was still there and she had her phone.

It was just that I almost always knew where she was.

Then I reminded myself that I was the one who had run off without a word.

It served me right that she had done the same.

I slowed my pace and followed the path down to the garden area.

The freshly bloomed flowers, mostly in lilac and white were beautiful.

But I barely saw them in my quest to find Emma.

With every step, I was more and more worried about her.

Reaching the end of the garden path, I turned and started back toward the hotel.

It was time for me to take the next step.

I opened my phone and turned on the locator.

Emma was close by. She was near the edge of the lake.

Tamping down my alarm, I made my way toward her.

And there she was.

Standing next to the shore, looking out over the lake.

Caught in the breeze coming off the water, her hair fluttered around her.

My heart caught in my throat.

Going on impulse, I broke off one of the white roses and took it with me as I walked toward her.

She turned and looked at me as I neared her.

I immediately knew that something was wrong.

My spirits plummeted.

54

EMMA

*W*aves rolled gently onto the shore. I tucked my hands into my jacket pocket and shivered against the chilly wind.

A mother duck and her three babies waddled to the edge of the water and walked into the waves.

The mother duck dipped into the water and the babies tried their hand at it, shaking their heads as they tried to stay steady in the water.

A ferry boat floated slowly toward the island, bringing crowds of day tourists to the island.

I felt Harrison coming up behind me before I saw him. I turned and watched him, trying to force a smile onto my lips.

But I saw him miss a step and knew that he knew something was wrong.

"Good morning," he said, coming to stand next to me.

"Hi." It was almost painful to see him.

That's how it was to fall in love with someone who wasn't available.

I'd gotten swept away in the moment. My heart had mistaken a fake wedding... a fake honeymoon... for a real one.

"Sorry I disappeared," he said. "I went to get us coffee and it took longer than I intended."

I nodded.

"The coffee got cold," he said. "So I brought you this instead." He held up a white rose.

My hands trembled as I took it from him and held it close to my chest.

I closed my eyes and forced myself to breathe.

"Thank you, "I murmured.

He put his hands in his own pockets and stood next to me, looking out across the water.

"I was wondering what we should do today."

"I think we should go home." I wondered if he could hear the way I had to force myself to say the words. If he could hear the pain that saying the words caused me.

"Something wrong?" he asked.

"No," I lied, shaking my head. "I just need to get back."

"Okay," he said, but didn't move.

I brought the rose to my nose and inhaled deeply. It smelled so good. So sweet. Bittersweet.

"Are you sure?" he asked.

"Yes."

"Did I do something wrong?"

"No." I shook my head. "You didn't do anything wrong."

I couldn't tell him that I was the one who had messed up.

I had messed up and fallen in love with him.

I'd taken him away from the girl he loved.

He had sacrificed himself to keep me from being deported.

And now I had to fix it.

Even if it broke my heart into a thousand pieces.

55

HARRISON

*B*randon Barrett not only worked for Skye Travels, but he also lived on Mackinac Island.

One of the luckiest men alive if you asked me. It helped that he was married to Annabelle Lawson, one of the richest women in Texas. The waste management company her grandfather had left her had flourished under her watch.

Noah, in that uncanny way he had, had taken advantage of the opportunity when Brandon, one of his pilots, had expressed an interest in living on Mackinac Island.

Instead of losing a good pilot, Noah had left a small airplane on the island with a pilot available at a moment's notice.

As a result, by the time we got our things packed up and got to the airport, Brandon was there ready to fly us south.

Sitting next to Emma, not being able to touch her, not knowing what had happened to put a wall between us, made for a long flight.

As we flew back to Houston, I replayed every minute since we'd decided to get married, but I couldn't come up with a single thing that might have triggered such a response.

Brandon took the plane in for a perfect landing at the

Houston airport, then taxied over to the Skye Travels private terminal.

A few minutes later, after he secured the plane, he came back to open the door.

"I just spoke to Noah," he said. "Seems congratulations are in order."

"Thank you," I said.

Emma just gave a quick nod and tight smile.

Things, it seemed were going from bad to worse.

"Well," Brandon said. "I hope things go as well for you as they did for me and Annabella. We honeymooned on the island as well."

"I'm sure they will," I said.

We unhooked our belts and followed Brandon down the steps to the tarmac where a car was waiting.

I gave the chauffeur Emma's address.

"It's a beautiful day," I said as we settled into the back seat of the car.

"Yes," Emma agreed.

The long flight had done nothing to lighten her mood.

So I left her alone until we reached her condo.

She said nothing as the chauffeur unloaded both her luggage and mine and we rolled it all into her house.

Alone at last, I took her hands.

"Emma," I said. "Please talk to me. Tell me what I did to make you so unhappy."

"You didn't do anything," she said, not meeting my gaze.

"Something changed," I said. "between last night and this morning. Surely you owe it to me to at least give me some idea what thing is."

"Alright," she said. "but I need a moment."

Torturing me. That's what she was doing. And I had no idea what I'd done to deserve it.

Ten minutes later she came back with two bottles of water. Sitting on the sofa, she handed me one.

I unscrewed the top and drank, then sat beside her.

"I realized," she said, finally. "that I had taken this ruse too far."

Her words stung. I'd begun to think of our marriage as something more than a ruse.

"In what way?"

"I don't know yet," she said. "I need to take some time. To think about it."

"What would you like me to do?"

She met my gaze then and I saw such pain her eyes.

"I'd like you to give me time and space to sort it all out."

So that was it then. She wanted me to leave her alone.

56

EMMA

*H*ad I thought it all through a little more, I would have found another way home.

Flying back with Harrison at my side... riding in the car next to him... having him come inside and insist on knowing what he had done wrong... it was all torture of the worse kind.

I couldn't... wouldn't... tell him that I knew about Christy.

Knowing about it was bad enough, but to have him talk to me about it would have been more than I could bear.

So I put up a wall around myself and waited for him to go.

The man was persistent, that much I could say for certain.

I had to all but tell him that I wanted him to leave.

Then when he did go, I watched in miserable silence as he rolled his luggage outside and waited for an Uber to come and pick him up.

I couldn't stay here. The thought of returning to work at Skye Designs was unbearable.

After the Uber picked Harrison up and drove him out of my life, I paced the floor of my condo.

I didn't even unpack. I needed to do something.

I couldn't be with Harrison and I couldn't be here without him.

I had no one to talk to about it. No family. No close friends. Just me.

Picking up my phone, I scrolled through my contacts.

My finger hovered over Noah's name.

Was that the answer?

I kept scrolling, but after reaching the end of my contacts, I sat on my sofa and stared at Noah's number.

Maybe I should have told Harrison what I had seen. That I knew about his girlfriend.

I just hadn't been able to bear the pain of hearing him talk about her.

I decided to send Noah a text first.

ME: *This is Emma. Do you have a minute to talk?*

NOAH: *Sure. You can call me.*

Taking a deep breath, I dialed his number before I could change my mind.

"Noah Worthington."

"Noah. Hi. This is Emma."

"Hi Emma. Is everything okay? Are you still at Mackinac?"

"No. I um... I changed my mind."

"About what?"

I felt like I was on a train with a hundred cars and even if I wanted to stop it, I couldn't. It had gotten out of control.

"Can you fly me to Vancouver?"

There was a moment of silence on the other end of the line.

"Where are you now?"

"I'm at home. In Houston."

"Where is Harrison?"

"I don't know. Home I guess."

"When do you want to leave?"

"Now." There. I'd done it. I'd gone and blown up my life. Nothing would ever be the same again.

"Are you sure about this?"

"Yes." I hoped he didn't hear the pain in my voice. The utter hopelessness. "I'm sure."

"Can you get to the airport?"

"Of course," I said. "Thank you."

I disconnected the line and sat holding my phone.

Now that it was done, I was wishing I could rewind the day and start it all over again.

This was not how I'd wanted my day... my life... to go.

But it was for the best. I could take care of everything from Vancouver. I could sell my condo furnished. Seek an annulment.

Seek a license to practice architecture in Canada.

I would be starting over, but I could do it.

I would do it to in order to allow Harrison to be happy.

57

HARRISON

I stepped into my condo and dropped my keys on the little table beside my front door.

The wood floor gleamed and everything smelled fresh. The housekeeper had been there, leaving everything cleaned. I'd intentionally had it cleaned with the expectation that I would be bringing Emma home with me.

I would have left it up to her, of course. If she preferred to go home to her place, we would do that. I would have been okay with living anywhere with her. My place. Her place. A new place. Hell, I would have been okay with us living in a hotel.

As long as we were together I didn't care.

But instead of worrying about where we would live, I had to worry about what had happened. To say that I was stunned was an understatement.

I didn't know what had happened.

I rolled my suitcase into my bedroom and tossed it on the bed.

Running a hand through my hair, I stood there trying to decide my next move.

I needed a whiskey.

Going downstairs, I went to my bar and poured whiskey into a glass. I downed it.

I refilled my glass and drank this one more slowly as I walked back to my bedroom.

Sitting in the armchair in one corner of my room, I set the glass on the end table and opened my phone.

I checked my messages, first, out of habit. But I had no messages from Emma and that was all I cared about.

My cell phone battery was low, so I went to my suitcase, unzipped it, and tossed back the lid.

Normally much more organized, I just shrugged and dug through my clothes looking for my charger.

As I shoved aside shirts and socks my fingers brushed against a photograph.

It was a printed photograph of me and Christy, taken last Christmas.

I must have left it there after I returned from visiting her family over the holidays. Her brother had insisted on printing out some of the photos we had of each other and Christy had given me this one.

That was before everything with her had fallen apart.

The picture had apparently gotten left in my suitcase.

That visit to her parents' house had been the culmination of the end of our relationship. We'd been headed that way for longer than I liked to admit, so it wasn't much of a surprise.

I was thankful that things had ended with her when they did, leaving me available to be with Emma.

My phone chimed, jarring me out of a not so pleasant memory.

But it wasn't Emma. It was Noah.

"What's happened?" he asked.

I knew he knew.

It made sense that he would, since it was his private airline company that had flown us home.

"Emma needed to come home."

"I got that," he said. "I don't go into the office every day anymore, but it only takes one phone call. I'm asking why Emma is returning to Vancouver."

"What? What do you mean?"

"Emma," Noah said. "She's headed to Vancouver."

"No." I fell onto the chair, the photograph of me and my old girlfriend falling to the floor. "She's at her house."

"No. She is on her way to the airport. Brandon is taking her with him back to Mackinac. Then flying her to Vancouver in the morning."

"Why?"

Noah was silent a moment.

"I called to ask you," he said.

"When did she leave?"

"I'm guessing they're taking off right about now."

"Damn. Damn. Damn."

"Harrison?"

"Yes?" I forced myself to focus.

"Get your act together."

58

EMMA

I didn't stay at the Grand Hotel. It would have been too painful.

I stayed at the downtown Chippewa Hotel.

Standing on the deck overlooking Lake Huron, I watched one of the ferries bump up against the dock. Tourists stood on the boat, eager to come ashore.

There was no one else out here on the deck and that suited me just fine.

The sunset splashed across the sky in streaks of reds and golds blending with shades of pink and yellow. The color reflected off the blue shimmering water coming ashore in gentle waves.

I couldn't stop thinking about my picnic with Harrison. How we'd sat on the shore watching the waves come in.

Tomorrow I would be back in Vancouver. And as much as that wasn't what I wanted, I would be eternally grateful to Noah Worthington for his kindness.

Harrison's whole extended family had been kind.

It made it worse that I had no family of my own, extended or otherwise.

It was a reminder of what I was missing in life. As long as I buried myself in my work, I didn't have to think about what other people were doing outside of work.

Work was my life.

Or it had been until I had married Harrison.

I rested my chin on my hands and watched the tourists as they got off the boat. They must be coming to stay the night because they had loads of luggage with them.

The speck of a small airplane grew larger as it flew toward the island.

As it passed overhead, the deafening sound brought a rush of memories. Bittersweet.

Though it saddened me, it made my heart beat faster.

I had so many memories with Harrison. Good memories.

And for me everything had been genuine.

I wasn't even sure where the line blurred into a marriage of convenience to a real marriage.

There was no definitive point. It had just sort of happened. Like one of the waves coming in. Where did they start? No one could say. But when they crashed against the shore, everything changed.

I stood there on the deck with nowhere to be and no one to talk to. And even though I'd been alone most of my life, I never felt alone. Not until now. Not like this.

I'd never felt so alone.

I'd crashed my life and now I had to start over from scratch.

And all because of a paperwork error.

That's how it worked, I supposed. Marry in haste, repent in leisure. Was there an idiom for falling in love in haste? I should write one.

Fall in love in haste, for the heart to break.

Fall in love in haste, for a state of disgrace.

A poet I was not.

Good thing I knew how to design buildings.

I straightened. I was a good architect. Very good.

I could do this.

I would start again and be successful.

It was time to get some sleep. In the morning I would start a new life. I could be anyone I wanted to be.

With the cool evening wind tousling my hair about my shoulders, I turned to go back inside.

With a little gasp, I froze.

Harrison stood in the doorway.

I swayed.

I was hallucinating.

59

HARRISON

*A*fter a whirlwind trip to Houston, I was back on Mackinac Island. One of the strangest days I'd ever had.

I'd gone from being head over heels in love with my new wife to crashing and burning in heartbreak.

And right now the object of that heartbreak was about to faint.

I took the steps that closed the distance between us and caught her just as she swayed.

"Harrison?"

"I didn't know you were prone to fainting." I was on one knee and she was sitting on my thigh.

"I wasn't fainting," she said, but she looked rather pale to me and her hands trembled.

"If you insist," I said.

"What are you doing here?" she asked, still trembling, but the color was coming back in her cheeks.

"Finding you."

"But how?" She looked utterly and charmingly confused.

"You might recall that it's my job to keep up with you."

Now she looked rather vexed.

"You're not supposed to be here."

"You're here, aren't you?"

"What does that mean?" Her fingers toyed with the hair at the back of my neck that nearly brushed my collar.

"Since I'm here, maybe you could give me an explanation…. A real one."

"You should be with Christy."

"Christy?" Now it was my turn to be utterly confused. "How do you know about Christy?"

"I saw the photo." She took a deep breath. "In your suitcase."

The photograph in my suitcase. The one I'd accidentally left there.

"I didn't mean to see it." Her words came out in a rush. "But you weren't there and it was an accident."

"My love," I said. "Christy and I broke up. Officially after the holidays. It was long overdue."

"But the photo…"

"Left in my luggage and forgotten, I can assure you."

"But—"

I placed a finger over her lips.

"Emma," I said, letting the love I felt for her flood through me. "It's you. You're the one for me." I gazed into her lovely green eyes. Shifted her on my knee.

"You're sure?" she asked.

"Emma." I tucked a strand of hair, blown into her eyes by the wind, behind her neck and went with my gut.

"I'm in love with you. Will you be my wife? For real?"

She leaned in and kissed me.

"I am your wife. For real. I never pretended."

"Me either."

I brought her close and kissed her.

For real.

60

EMMA

*S*tanding on the longest porch in the world, I felt like the luckiest girl in the world.

The deep mournful sound of the ferry horn was delightful.

Lilacs in clay pots mixed the scent of the recent rain.

My wedding ring gleamed in the morning sunlight as I set my coffee cup on the railing.

Harrison brought my right hand up to his lips and kissed the back of my fingers.

We'd been inseparable since last night when he'd proposed to me a second time.

I hadn't thought I could be happier, but it seemed happiness had no bounds.

After our whirlwind trip to Houston and back, we still had four days left on the island before we went back to work.

"How do you feel about history?" Harrison asked.

"History? That's an odd question."

He grinned. "We could walk up to the fort and check out one of the reenactments."

"Wasn't that part of the War of 1812?"

"Ah. Very good. You never cease to impress me."

I shrugged, but was secretly pleased that he was impressed.

"You know," I said. "They say that those of us who move to America know more American history than those who were born here."

"Probably true." He straightened and looked out toward the horizon. "Is that a yes?"

"Sure. I don't mind a little history."

Truth was I didn't care what we did as long as we were together.

I would be happy if I never had to be away from him again.

He pulled me close, holding me in front of him, resting his chin on the top of my head.

"We have some things to figure out," I said.

"We have a lifetime to figure out."

I sighed. He was right.

We did have a lifetime to figure out.

Day by day.

Moment by moment.

And this was one of those moments.

Harrison was good for me.

He kept me grounded.

Reminded me to savor the moment and not worry so much about having everything in life planned out ahead of time.

It was impossible to plan everything anyway.

Only last week, I never would have guessed in a million years that I would standing on Mackinac Island with my husband—the man of my dreams.

Two white egrets swooped low and flew together toward the lake.

That was how I felt with Harrison.

Wild and free. I turned and looked back up at him.

He hadn't shaved yet, but the slightly rugged look fit him.

"I love you," I said.
"I love you," he said without hesitation.
Then he kissed me.

61

NOELLE

*S*nuggling into my new long wool coat, I stepped out of the subway and headed toward the park. The white clouds were banked and the first flakes of the season's first snowfall were falling.

I turned my face up toward the sky, letting the wispy flakes fall on my face.

It was near noon on a Wednesday morning. I'd been in Boston over a week.

I'd be meeting with Ben tomorrow about taking some flights for him, but other than setting that up, I'd had a leisurely week. It was a strange feeling not having anything to do. I'd had a weekend like that here and there over my life, but never a whole week.

I wouldn't say I could get used to it, but oddly enough, I hadn't minded.

I reached the fountain in Boston Common and stopped to watch the snowflakes landing in the water.

A calmness had settled over me the past few days. I was at peace with myself.

I realized I didn't have to decide my future right away. I could take my time.

A man with a neatly trimmed silver beard, also in a wool coat, walked passed and smiled at me.

I smiled back. This was what I liked about Boston. People said the south was friendly, but I'd found the Boston to be open and accepting.

I wandered aimlessly along the walkway, wondering how things might have looked hundreds of years ago when the city was young.

A man sitting on a park bench a few yards ahead stood up and faced me. I didn't pay him much mind. I just continued my stroll.

Then he stepped out in front of me.

And I was face to face with Quinn Worthington.

I froze, standing a few feet in front of him.

"Hello Noelle," he said, with that little grin I'd fallen in love with.

"Quinn? What are you doing here?"

"Looking for you."

"But…"

"How did I find you?"

I nodded, my head reeling.

"You told me," he said.

I tilted my head to the side. "No. I don't think so."

He took a step forward.

"You told me that Boston was your favorite place out of all the places you'd ever lived."

"I did, didn't I?" A snowflake fell on my eyelashes and I blinked it away.

He nodded. "You did."

I swallowed and forced myself to think.

"I didn't know you were engaged," I said.

"I didn't either."

"Makenna said—"

"Makenna is a troubled teenager who doesn't know what she's talking about." He said the words quickly.

I shook my head.

"I told Father about you. I told him ten years ago that I'd met the only girl for me and I told him he'd just hired that very same girl. I'm sure he and my mother talked about it. They talk about everything."

"I don't understand. Makenna…"

"Makenna must have overheard them talking. About me and you. But she didn't know that you were you. She thought you were someone else."

Unless she was just being mean. He didn't have to say it for it to be true.

He closed the distance between us and put his hands on my arms to pull me close.

"Noelle," he said. "You've always been the only girl for me."

My heart was beating so fast, I wondered if he could hear it.

He tilted my chin up so that I could look into those blue eyes with the emerald green streaks.

"I waited for you," he said.

My breath hitched.

"You waited for me all those years?" Maybe he was insane. "You didn't even know who I was."

"I knew everything I needed to know. I knew that you were my soul mate. And…"

He pressed his lips against mine.

"And?" I asked, looked up at him through my lashes.

"And the day I saw you walking across the tarmac I decided to let you go. To move on. Maybe that girl walking towards me had possibilities."

"That girl was me." I shivered, but it wasn't from the cold.

"Yes. I set you free, but you were already there. You know the saying, right?"

"If you let something go and it doesn't come back, it was never yours. If it comes back to you, it's yours."

"Something like that."

"Noelle," he said. "Will you be mine?"

My heart swelled. I could feel the pieces fitting back together again.

"I've always been yours."

Kissing me, he put his arms around me and I put my arms around his shoulders.

He lifted my feet off the ground and twirled me around.

Then he put an arm beneath my knees and lifted me off the ground.

"Let's get out of here," he whispered against my lips."

Then after another long kiss, he turned and carried me toward the subway.

Loved Reading about Emma and Harrison?

Turn the page for a preview of
Billionaire's Unexpected Landing...

BILLIONAIRE'S UNEXPECTED LANDING PREVIEW

SARAH LAWRENCE

I didn't wear the air pods for music. I wore them to keep out the noise from the jet. I had a good first-class seat and no one bothered me, but I needed the quiet to work.

Absently taking a sip of chilled, bottled water, I changed another word on one of my PowerPoint slides. Just one word. Intrinsic to innate.

I was fiddling with it too much. I needed to leave it alone.

But I was nervous. I was a contender for a promotion. It was down to me and one other pharmaceutical representative. A guy by the name of Tyler Lexton.

I'd never even met the guy, but in my mind, he had the advantage because he already lived in Houston and the company we both worked for was based out of Houston.

I had, however, looked him up. He had two years more experience than I did. Another advantage on his side.

I took a deep breath and glanced out the window.

We were descending already.

I checked my watch. Then my electronic ticket.

Something was wrong.

I closed my Macbook Pro and slid it into my leather computer bag.

We were still at least an hour out of Houston. This wasn't my usual route—most of my flights had been in the western region of the country, but I had flown enough to know when a plane was going in for a landing.

I looked for a flight attendant, but, of course, no one was around.

Then the pilot came over the speaker.

"Due to a mechanical issue, we are making an unexpected landing at the airport in the fine city of Abilene, Texas. Don't worry, though, folks, it's not serious. It's just a precaution. We'll have you back in the air in no time at all."

I leaned back in my seat, straightening my black pencil skirt.

I'd been flying at least once a week for years. It had taken me one year after I'd graduated college and taken my first job as a drug representative to get promoted to a territory sales position. I'd gone from regional to territory just that quick.

The next step up was divisional sales manager, but those positions were competitive.

This *precaution* was going to make me late. My presentation wasn't until morning, but if I missed dinner tonight, I would never recover from the disadvantage.

The company, Clinical Pharm Distributing, was hosting a cocktail dinner with the executives and us two contenders. Me and Tyler.

Since I had Wi-Fi, I sent my supervisor a text. Zachary was a successful man who could have moved up the corporate ladder even more, but he had a family in Los Angeles. He and his husband had adopted a little girl. And the next step up would have put him relocating in Houston.

ME: *There is a problem. My plane is landing in Abilene.*
ZACHARY: *Why?*

ME: *A mechanical... precaution.*

ZACHARY: *You'll be late.*

It didn't bother me that Zachary wasn't worried about the problem with the airplane. He was no nonsense. He'd sent me here for an interview and he expected me to be there. On time.

ME: *Nothing I can do.*

ZACHARY: *Hold on. Let me check on something.*

ME: *Not going anywhere.*

I watched as the plane landed on a little runway in what looked like the middle of absolutely nowhere.

Zachary texted back as we taxied down the runway.

ZACHARY: *There are no more flights out of Abilene today. At least none that will get you to Houston.*

This was it. I was going to lose my one time opportunity for a position that rarely came open. No telling how long I would have to wait for an opportunity like this to come open again.

ZACHARY: *Don't worry. I've gotten it taken care of.*

Seriously? Nobody had that much influence over the airlines. Not even Zachary.

LUKE WORTHINGTON

So much for my plans for the evening.

It was a beautiful October day and the evening promised to be just as beautiful. Already I could see the full moon high in the sky. The moon on one side of me and the sun on the other. There was no job in the world with a better view. Wouldn't trade it for anything.

Just when I was preparing to fly back to Houston from a drop off in Fort Worth, I got a call from Father. My father, Quinn Worthington, ran Skye Travels. Skye Travels, established by my grandfather Noah Worthington, was one of the biggest private airlines in the country.

I'd always known I would be a pilot and I'd always known I

would fly for Skye Travels. But my father ran the company with an iron fist. The funny thing about Father was that he wasn't even a pilot. Grandpa was and he still flew on occasion. They didn't make them like him anymore.

Quinn didn't make the schedule, but when he said the schedule needed to be changed, it got changed. No questions asked.

A flight from L.A. had made an unexpected landing, so I was making a detour through Abilene, Texas. I'd been there once. Maybe. I'd flown to so many little airports, only a few of them were memorable. Most of them just ran together.

Father had already submitted my travel plan, so all I had to do was to go through the preflight checklist.

I didn't mind. Not really. But I'd planned to have dinner with my cousin, Daniel and his girlfriend. They were driving through and would only be here the one night. We'd planned on having dinner. Looks like dinner was going to be pushed back a bit.

I'd offered a million times to fly him wherever he wanted to go, but my cousin insisted on driving.

Personally I saw no reason to drive when I could fly. It was so much faster and so much more relaxing. No dodging traffic up here in the sky.

I dreaded the day when that changed and the sky was clogged with traffic. It was coming. Maybe not in my lifetime, but some day.

I taxied out onto the runway and waited my turn to take off.

I knew the Fort Worth airport like the back of my hand. This one and the Houston airport where Skye Travels was based.

Thirty minutes later I was in the air headed to Abilene. A short flight to pick up one passenger. I checked my notes. Sarah Lawrence.

I didn't recognize the name.

I had a few people that asked for me and I flew them frequently. Then there were others, like this one, that were just one time customers. They either had some kind of emergency or they were splurging for a special occasion.

The latter were always fun. The former not so much.

Father hadn't given me any additional information about Sarah. No special requests from her. So I entertained myself by filling in the gaps.

It was a short flight on short notice. I'd bet money that she was one of the emergency passengers.

As the wheels touched down at the Abilene airport, I put on my pilot's cap—standard uniform for Skye Travels—and prepared myself to pick up a distraught female. Probably an older woman, if I had to guess. Probably had an adult child in Houston, a professional who had sent for her. Maybe they were having a baby and wanted Granny there.

After a smooth landing, if I did have to say so myself, I taxied over to the private terminal and came to a stop.

A woman wearing a solid black pencil skirt that looked like she'd been melted and poured into, stepped out and started walking toward me. In most definite high heels that gave her a seductive walk that I doubted she was doing on purpose.

Well. If this was my passenger, she was most definitely not someone's granny.

Keep reading Billionaire's Unexpected Landing…

ABOUT THE AUTHOR

Kathryn Kaleigh is the author of over seventy novels, over one hundred short stories, and many collections.

kathrynkaleigh.com